Clint spoke when the man on the table opened his eyes. "We've got some bad news for you. You're going to live."

The man laughed, which caused him some pain, and he winced. "That's bad news?" he asked.

"It is for you," Clint said. "See, the town is up in arms about the woman who got killed. Seems they want to hang somebody for it. So guess what?" Clint laughed and said, "We're going to give them you." He paused to let that sink in for a while. "I don't think the townspeople will care that you didn't actually kill her yourself, once we tell them you were with the Bacas. They're just looking for somebody to string up. Now—you sure you don't remember where the Baca brothers were going from here?"

DON'T MISS THESE
ALL-ACTION WESTERN SERIES
FROM THE BERKLEY PUBLISHING GROUP

THE GUNSMITH by J. R. Roberts
>   Clint Adams was a legend among lawmen, outlaws, and ladies. They called him . . . the Gunsmith.

LONGARM by Tabor Evans
>   The popular long-running series about U.S. Deputy Marshal Long—his life, his loves, his fight for justice.

LONE STAR by Wesley Ellis
>   The blazing adventures of Jessica Starbuck and the martial arts master, Ki. Over eight million copies in print.

SLOCUM by Jake Logan
>   Today's longest-running action Western. John Slocum rides a deadly trail of hot blood and cold steel.

THE GUNSMITH

145

GILLETT'S RANGERS

J. R. ROBERTS

JOVE BOOKS, NEW YORK

GILLETT'S RANGERS

A Jove Book / published by arrangement with
the author

PRINTING HISTORY
Jove edition / January 1994

ISBN: 0-515-11285-2

A JOVE BOOK®
Jove Books are published by The Berkley Publishing Group,
200 Madison Avenue, New York, New York 10016.
JOVE and the "J" design are trademarks
belonging to Jove Publications, Inc.

PRINTED IN THE UNITED STATES OF AMERICA

10 9 8 7 6 5 4 3 2 1

THE GUNSMITH

145

GILLETT'S RANGERS

ONE

Christmas without snow was not quite the same for Clint Adams, but there was very little chance of seeing snow in New Mexico, even in the winter.

December twenty-fifth was still a week away, and Clint was traveling through New Mexico to get back to Texas. He wanted to spend Christmas in Labyrinth, where he had some friends. In the past, Christmas had been just another day for Clint, but in recent years he'd started to look at it differently. True, he had no family to spend it with, but he did have a lot of friends spread across the country, friends he had made during all his years of traveling.

He'd known a lot of women, too, over the years, and could think of several he wouldn't have minded spending Christmas with. Unfortunately, he didn't know where most of them were.

Two of them were lady bounty hunters, and they could have been anywhere. One was named Anne

Archer, who did her hunting in the company of her two partners, Sandy Spillane and Katy Littlefeather. The other was Lacy Dalton, who worked with a man named Jake Benteen. Either woman would have made a wonderful holiday companion, but given his choice, Clint probably would have chosen Anne. They seemed to have the most in common, and she seemed to be the one woman he connected with the most.

Of course, that was because Joanna Morgan was dead, and had been dead for many years.

Clint knew he was about a mile outside of Socorro, New Mexico. He had been riding all day without resting, and he was looking forward to a beer, a meal, and a night in bed. When he saw someone lying by the road up ahead, he was afraid that those pleasures were going to have to be put off.

Clint rode up close and looked down at the man. It was obvious that he was still alive, but he wasn't moving much. There were drag marks behind him, so either someone had dragged him there or the man had managed to pull himself up to the road where he could be seen.

Clint dismounted and crouched over the man. He had a pretty bad bump on his head and some sort of wound on his arm, probably from a knife. The blood had dried, so the wound wasn't that bad. There was no telling yet if the man's head injury was serious.

The man was lying on his side, so Clint rolled him over onto his back. As the light of the dying sun struck the man's face, he inadvertently flinched.

"Well, good," Clint said aloud, "you're still alive."

"I don't feel alive," the man said. He opened his eyes, then immediately shut them against the sun's glare.

"Let's turn you around so the sun's not in your eyes," Clint said.

He helped the man move into a position where he'd be able to open his eyes.

"I want to sit up," the injured man said, "but I'm gonna need help."

"Wait a few minutes," Clint said. "Let me check you out first."

Clint examined the man and decided that there were no broken bones or limbs.

"All right," Clint said, "you can sit, but let's go slow."

He helped the man into a sitting position, then fetched his canteen from his saddle.

"Drink it slowly."

The man took a few swallows and then handed the canteen back.

"Feel like standing?" Clint asked.

"No," the man said, "but let's give it a try, anyway."

Clint helped the man struggle to his feet.

"Whoa!" the man said and reeled as a dizzy spell struck him.

"Okay, okay," Clint said, holding him tightly, "let's go back down. Obviously standing up right now is not a good idea."

"I agree with that," the man said. When he was sitting back on the ground, he said, "Wow, everythin' just started goin' around."

"All right, we can sit here awhile until you feel like moving," Clint said. "Maybe we should introduce ourselves. My name is Clint Adams."

"Gillett," the man said, with his head in his hands, "James Gillett. I'm with the Texas Rangers."

"The Rangers?" Clint said in surprise. "Aren't you a little out of your jurisdiction?"

"I don't know," Gillett said, lifting his head and looking at Clint. "Where am I?"

"Whoa," Clint said after a moment, "you really *were* hit on the head hard, weren't you?"

TWO

After about fifteen minutes or so, Clint helped Gillett move further off the road and decided that they'd camp there for the night.

"I'd rather ride into town," Gillett said.

"So would I," Clint said, "but I don't think you're up to it."

"Well, you don't have to stay with me," Gillett said. "You could leave me some supplies."

"And then what?" Clint asked. "You'll walk to town in the morning?"

"You could send someone back for me."

"It's better that I just stay here with you," Clint said, "unless you don't want my company for some reason, Mr. Gillett."

"No reason I can think of," Gillett said, "and the name's Jim."

"Clint," the Gunsmith said. "You fancy some coffee?"

5

"I could use it, and somethin' to eat."

"When's the last time you ate?"

Gillett looked at him and said, "I'm the guy you just had to tell where he was, remember? My head's still a little fuzzy for hard questions like when's the last time I ate."

"Okay," Clint said. "Get some rest, and here." He handed the man his canteen. "You might want to wash some of that dirt off your face."

"With your water?"

"We're an hour from town, Jim," Clint reminded him. "We'll have plenty of water come morning. Besides, I keep a spare canteen so I can always make coffee."

"Okay," Gillett said, "thanks."

"You might want to work on your arm, too," Clint said, "unless you'd rather I did it."

"That's okay," Gillett said, "I can handle it."

"Knife wound?"

Gillett frowned and said, "I think so. I'll know better when my head clears."

Clint left the man spilling water onto a handkerchief and scrubbing dirt and sand off his face. He built a fire and put on a pot of coffee, then checked his saddlebags to see what he had left to eat.

"Got some bacon and beans left," he told Gillett.

"Sounds good to me," Gillett said. "My head's clearin' some. I don't think I've eaten in a couple of days."

"I'll have it ready pretty quick," Clint said. "I'm kind of hungry myself."

While Clint was cooking, Gillett asked, "You been on the trail awhile?"

"Too long."

"Guess you were kind of lookin' forward to a hotel bed tonight, huh?"

"Ah," Clint said, "I've been sleeping on the ground so long I probably wouldn't have been able to sleep on a mattress, anyway."

When the coffee was ready, Clint poured two cups and handed one to Gillett. They sat drinking coffee and listening to the bacon spit.

"You did say your name was Clint Adams, didn't you?" Gillett asked after a long period of silence.

"That's right."

"My head . . ." Gillett said, pointing to it, as if Clint didn't know where it was. "I wasn't thinking too clearly when you made the introduction. You *are* the one they call the Gunsmith, aren't you?"

"That's right," Clint said.

In the past he would have flinched or grimaced, but these days he had taken to answering the question as simply as possible.

"Where were you headed when you found me, Clint?" Gillett asked.

"Socorro."

"And after that?"

"On into Texas. A town called Labyrinth."

"I think I know it."

"I've got some friends there," Clint said. "Thought that's where I'd hole up for Christmas."

"Christmas?" Gillett said. "Is Christmas comin'?"

"About a week away," Clint said. "Your head still fuzzy?"

"No, no," Gillett said, "I've just been . . . on the trail

so long I lost track of time. Christmas, huh?"

"Don't you have some family you'd like to be with for the holidays?"

"No," Gillett said, his face darkening, "no family. I used to think the Rangers were my family, but . . ."

The man trailed off, and Clint took that to mean that he didn't want to discuss it any further.

"How about you?" Gillett asked. "Any family to speak of?"

"No," Clint said. "No family."

"Guess that makes us orphans, huh? When it comes to the holidays?"

"I guess so," Clint said.

When the food was ready, he dished it out and handed a plate to Gillett, who ate ravenously. Clint was hungry, but obviously not as starved as the Texas Ranger was, so he ate sparingly so that there'd be more for Gillett.

"That was good," Gillett said, "only I noticed you didn't eat much."

"I ate enough," Clint said. "I'm ready for more coffee."

"So am I."

Clint cleaned up, then made a fresh pot of coffee and handed Gillett a cup. Armed with one himself, he sat down next to the man.

"How's your head?"

"It's fine," Gillett said. "Still aches, but for the most part it's okay."

"Pretty clear?"

"Clear enough."

"Clear enough to tell me what happened to you?" Clint asked.

Gillett took a minute to think. Clint wondered if the man was thinking if he *could* tell him what happened, or simply if he *wanted* to.

"Yeah," Gillett said finally, "yeah, I think I could do that."

THREE

"Have you ever heard of the Baca brothers—Enofre and Abran?" Gillett asked.

"Can't say that I have, no," Clint said.

"Well, they're from Mexico and they're killers, both of 'em," Gillett said, "and for some reason they seem to like to do their killin' in Texas."

"Guess they don't like to shit where they eat," Clint said.

Gillett gave Clint a strange look and then said, "That's a real good way of putting it. I never thought of it that way."

"So you were assigned to them?" Clint asked.

"No," Gillett said, "that's just it. *Nobody* was assigned to track them down, and when I asked about it, I was told to stay away from them."

"Why?"

"I don't know why," Gillett said, "and I couldn't find out."

10

"So what did you do?"

"I waited for them to hit again," Gillett said, "and then I started tracking them."

"All the way into New Mexico?"

"That's right," Gillett said. "They only come into Texas to satisfy their thirst for blood, and then they ride back out. Besides, it's not like they were going into Mexico. They're still in this country."

"Still," Clint said, "you are a *Texas* Ranger."

"It don't matter," Gillett said, shaking his head. "Somebody's gotta stop those boys from killin', and I volunteered myself for the job."

"So what happened here?" Clint asked. "Did they ambush you?"

"*Somebody* ambushed me," Gillett said. "Took my money and my gun—my badge, too. But if it was them, they would have killed me."

"That makes sense."

"So I think I was just careless," Gillett said. "I was concentrating so hard on tracking them that some common thief or thieves must have got the jump on me."

"Probably gave them a scare when they saw your badge," Clint said.

"Didn't scare them so much that they didn't take it," Gillett pointed out. He touched the back of his head and added, "I'm surprised I ain't dead, anyway, even if it wasn't the Baca boys."

"Maybe they just didn't feel comfortable killing a lawman," Clint said. "Some outlaws are like that, you know."

"I know," Gillett said. "Guess I should be grateful for that."

When they finished their coffee, Clint said, "Why don't you get some sleep?"

"What are you gonna do?"

"I'll stand watch for a while," Clint said. "I don't think it's necessary, but maybe I'll just do it for the first few hours."

"We could share the watch and keep it on all night," Gillett said.

"I don't think so," Clint said. "I don't think you're up to that. I'll just stay awake for a few hours."

"It don't seem fair, is all," Gillett said.

"Don't worry about it," Clint said. "After this we'll just consider that you owe me one."

"You got a deal, Clint," Gillett said, "but I don't think I'll be able to sleep very well."

"Give it a try," Clint said. Minutes later, Gillett was asleep.

Clint remained awake for a couple of hours, just in case the ambushers came back, but there really didn't seem to be much chance of that. If they hadn't finished Gillett off when they had the chance, why would they come back and do it now?

Finally, Clint bedded down, knowing full well that if someone did try to sneak into their camp, his big, black gelding, Duke, would sound some sort of an alarm.

FOUR

Clint woke first the next morning and had coffee on by the time Gillett woke up.

"Here," Clint said, handing him a cup of coffee.

Gillett sat up, blinking at the sun, and accepted the coffee.

"What was that I said about not being able to sleep?" he asked. "Whooee, I slept like a stone."

"Like the dead," Clint said.

Gillett flinched and said, "Don't even say that. If it wasn't for you, I probably would be dead."

"Well, drink up and then we'll get into Socorro," Clint said. "You can outfit yourself there."

"Not much chance of that," Gillett said. "I've got no money, remember?"

"Can't you send for some? From the Rangers?"

"Didn't I tell you?" he said. "I'm here unofficially. There's no way the Rangers are gonna send me any money. No, I'll just have to find another way."

13

"Well, listen—"

"Wait up!" Gillett said, putting his hand up. "I wasn't hinting for a loan."

"I know that," Clint said. "If I thought you were, I wouldn't even offer."

"Why don't we wait until we get to town to talk about that?" Gillett suggested. "Who knows, maybe I'll find the ones who ambushed me and get my gear back."

"Okay," Clint said, "if you want to play it that way, we'll wait."

After coffee they broke camp, and Clint stowed his gear away.

"We'll ride double," Clint said. "I think Duke can handle that for a mile or two."

"He looks like he could handle it for a hundred miles," Gillett said. "I don't think I've ever seen a better looking animal."

The big gelding's ears pricked up.

"Don't say that too often, or he might get to like it," Clint said.

He mounted up, then reached down and gave Gillett a hand up behind him. They rode like that to Socorro.

"You gon get yourself in trouble like that, you know," Pedro Hernandez said to his partner, José Santos.

"Like wha'?" José asked.

"Wearin' that badge," Pedro said, pointing to the Texas Ranger's star José was wearing on his shirt.

The two partners were in the cantina in Socorro, *Cantina Estralita*. They were seated at a table, drinking beer together. Early yesterday they had ambushed a man, meaning to steal his money and his horse. It turned out that the man was a Texas Ranger, so they took his badge, as well. Pedro said they should have killed him, but José said that by the time the man woke up they'd be in Mexico.

As it turned out, they had already stayed in Socorro longer than they intended. Pedro had found a woman, and José had found a poker game.

That was last night. Now they were sitting in the cantina having an early morning beer, and José was wearing the Texas Ranger's star on his chest.

"I like this star," José said. He looked down and polished it with his shirtsleeve.

"Were you wearin' that like that last night?" Pedro asked.

"Sure I was," José said. "I'm proud of it."

"You gon get in trouble," Pedro said again. "I think we should leave for Mexico now."

"We will leave soon," José said. "Very soon."

Pedro shook his head, thinking, José gon get himself in trouble . . . .

It was still early when Clint and Gillett rode down Socorro's main street.

"We should find the sheriff's office first," Clint said, "and let him know what happened. Maybe he'll know something."

"Let's get to a hotel first," Gillett said, and then he suddenly remembered that he had no money. "On second thought, maybe the sheriff's office would be better. Maybe he'll have them give me a room. You know, as a courtesy to a visiting lawman?"

"Maybe."

"Why don't you go to the hotel and get yourself a room?"

"Why don't I just come along with you to the sheriff's office?" Clint said. "I can back up your story. After all, you don't have a badge to show him."

"That's right," Gillett said from behind Clint. "You have a point—except for one thing."

"What's that?"

"Well, *you* haven't seen my badge, either," Gillett said. "What makes you believe me?"

"Let's just say I think hitting yourself over the head and lying by the side of the road would be a lot to go through if you were just trying to trick me into believing that you're a Texas Ranger."

"What if I made it up on the spot?"

"I don't think you were thinking that clearly at the time," Clint said. "Let's just say I'm willing to back up your story and leave it at that, okay?"

"Okay," Gillett said. "Let's find the man's office."

FIVE

They located the sheriff's office and dismounted in front of it. The town seemed to still be asleep, unless it was always like that.

"Quiet town," Gillett said, as if he were reading Clint's mind.

"Yeah."

Clint started for the door when Gillett said, "Ain't you gonna tie off your horse?"

"He's not going anywhere."

Gillett shrugged and followed Clint. They went inside and found an empty office.

"Not here," Gillett said.

"Wait," Clint said, and they both listened. From the back, where the cells were, came the sound of someone snoring.

"Unless he's got a prisoner," Clint said, "I think we found him."

They walked to the back and looked inside. There

17

were two cells, and in one of them a man was sleeping.
The door to the cell was wide open, so he obviously
was not a prisoner. From his appearance, though—
disheveled was putting it mildly—he could have been
a prisoner.

"Should we wake him up?" Gillett asked.

"Maybe we should just rob the bank while he's
asleep on the job," Clint said.

They looked at each other, and then Gillett said,
"Nah, let's wake him up."

"Okay."

Clint went into the cell to wake the man and decided to do it without touching him.

"Hey, Sheriff!"

The man did not move.

"Sheriff!" Clint called louder, but still the man didn't
respond.

"You're gonna have to shake him awake," Gillett
said.

"I hate to do that," Clint said. "I've known men who
have come out of a sound sleep shooting."

"Well," Gillett said, "shake him and stand back."

"Right."

Clint reached out, shook the man's shoulder, and
shouted, "Sheriff?"

He surprised them. Rather than jerking awake, he
simply opened his eyes and looked up at Clint, still,
however, without moving a muscle other than his
eyes.

"What do you want?"

"Well," Clint said, "are you the sheriff?"

"I am."

"We just rode into town," Clint said, "and we'd like to talk to you."

"About what?"

"If you'd come out to your office—"

"I'm comfortable here," the man said. "Go ahead and talk."

Clint frowned, then turned and gave Gillett a helpless look.

"Sheriff," Gillett said, coming forward into the cell, "my name is James Gillett. I'm a Texas Ranger."

"A little out of your bailiwick, ain't you, Ranger?" the man asked. He didn't question Gillett's claim at all, which Clint found odd. You would have thought he'd at least ask to see a badge.

"I guess I am," Gillett said.

"What can I do for you?"

"Well, yesterday—yesterday?" He looked at Clint, who nodded. They had figured out that the ambush must have happened early yesterday.

"Yesterday I was ambushed about a mile or two out of town," the Ranger went on. "They took my money, my outfit, and my badge."

"So?"

"Did you see anyone yesterday—"

"No."

"No what?" Gillett asked, getting annoyed now at the man's attitude.

"I didn't see nobody."

"You didn't see anybody . . . what?"

"Strange."

"It wouldn't have to be a stranger, Sheriff," Gillett said. "Some citizens of your fair town might have gotten it into their heads to ambush me."

"What do you want me to do?"

"Well," Gillett said, "for one thing you could get the hotel to give me a room, as a courtesy to another lawman."

"Mister," the supine sheriff said, "I can't even get the hotel to give *me* a room."

"Come on, Jim," Clint said. "I'll get you a room at the hotel. This is useless."

"You're right," Gillett said.

They started out and then Gillett stopped. He turned and saw that the sheriff's eyes had closed already.

"Sheriff!"

The man opened his eyes.

"If I find the men who ambushed me, you're gonna have to do something."

"Like what?"

Gillett glared at the man and said, "Like see that they're buried."

SIX

"Well, that was a waste of time," Gillett said. "What a poor excuse for a sheriff."

"It wasn't such a waste," Clint said.

"How do you mean?"

"You did tell him what happened, and you warned him about what might happen. He can't say later that he didn't know what was going on."

"You're right about that."

"Come on," Clint said, "We'll go over to the livery and get Duke taken care of, and then we'll go to the hotel and get a couple of rooms."

"I hate to rely on you again, Clint," Gillett said. "I'm gonna owe you so much before this is over."

"And don't think I won't collect, either," Clint said, smiling.

They walked to the livery and handed Duke over to a liveryman who looked almost as sleepy as the sheriff.

When they were ready to leave, Clint thought of something.

"Tell me, did anyone bring a horse in to sell yesterday?"

The liveryman, a grizzled veteran probably in his sixties, said, "As a matter of fact, somebody did."

"Did you buy it?"

"Nope."

"Why not?"

" 'Cause I knowed it was stole," the man said. He squinted at them and said, "It *was* stole, wasn't it?"

"It was stolen, all right," Clint said. "If it's the horse we're thinking of."

"A big gray with one white sock?" Gillett asked.

"That's the one."

"Where is it?"

"In the back," the man said. "Last stall on the right. "If'n it's yours, take it."

Clint and Gillett walked to the back to take a look.

"That's my horse," Gillett said excitedly. "They're here."

"Don't get too excited," Clint said. "All that means is that they were here yesterday."

"No," Gillett said, "they're here, I can feel it."

"Let's see if we can get a description from the old-timer," Clint said.

They found the liveryman again, and he told them that two Mexicans had tried to sell him the horse.

"Are their horses still here?" Gillett asked.

"Sure are," the man said.

Gillett looked at Clint and said, "They're still here, Clint."

"Let's go and find them, then."

"Hey," the liveryman yelled after them, "you kill them two fellers, their horses are mine, right?"

"Wait, wait," Clint said, grabbing Gillett's arm to slow his progress.

"What?"

"Let's still go to the hotel and check in, Jim," Clint said.

"Why?"

"Well, for one thing," Clint said, "I've got a spare gun I can loan you in my saddlebags."

"Well, give it to me."

"Let's go to the hotel, check in, and take a look at the gun. It has to be loaded, and I never use a gun without checking it first."

"Clint—"

"The last thing you want is to get killed because your gun misfired," Clint said. "Jim, those fellas aren't goin' anywhere in the next ten minutes. Come on."

"Okay, okay," Gillett said, "you're right. Let's go to the hotel."

They found the hotel and checked in. There was no problem getting two rooms.

"Have you got two Mexicans staying here?" Clint asked the clerk.

"Yes, we do," the clerk said, making a face. "They took one room."

"Have they checked out?"

"No," the clerk said, "but I won't mind when they do."

"You won't have to worry about that," Gillett said. "They won't *be* checking out."

They went upstairs to Clint's room. It wasn't necessary for them to go to Gillett's room since he had no belongings to drop off.

Clint fished out the spare gun, the Colt New Line that he carried as a belly gun.

"It's small," Gillett complained.

"Can you hit what you shoot at?" Clint asked.

"Most of the time."

"Then you won't have a problem with this," Clint said. "Besides, I'll give you my rifle as well."

Clint checked the action on the New Line, since it had been a while since he fired it, and then he loaded it and handed it to Gillett.

"All right," Clint said. "Let's go."

"You don't have to come along, Clint," Gillett said. "This ain't your fight."

"Ah, well," Clint said, "what would I do, just stand around and watch?"

Clint handed Gillett his rifle.

"I appreciate this," Gillett said.

"Besides," Clint added, "you're still not thinking right. You might miss."

"Oh, don't worry," Gillett said, "I'm not gonna miss."

Pedro Hernandez and José Santos both decided not to order another beer.

"I think you are right, Pedro," José said. "I think it is time to leave."

"It is about time," Pedro said.

They both stood up to leave, and Pedro said, "Uh, José?"

"Yes?"

"Are you gon to leave that badge on?"

José looked down at the badge on his chest.

"I like this badge, Pedro."

"I know, José," Pedro said, "but it is gon to get you in trouble. I told you not to take it."

"I wanted it," José said. "It is shiny."

"It is trouble."

"You are an old woman, Pedro."

"You will see, José," Pedro said warningly, "you will see."

SEVEN

"Where would you be this morning if you were two
Mexicans with money in their pockets?" Clint asked.

"Whatever money they have is mine," Gillett said,
"and there wasn't that much of it."

"That explains why they were trying to sell your
horse."

"I wonder if they sold my gun."

"Was it worth anything?"

"No," Gillett said. "It's not fancy, but it fits my
hand."

"Okay," Clint said, "let's make a choice then. Wom-
en or beer?"

"This early?" Gillett asked. "Probably women."

"All right, then," Clint said. "Let's find the local
whorehouse."

They were walking down the main street, just looking for someone to ask about the local whorehouse
when they saw two men step out of the cantina. The

sun was in just the right position in the sky to strike the two men as they came out the door, and both Clint and Gillett saw something on one of the men's chests.

"Did you see that?" Gillett asked.

"Yes," Clint said, "the sun's reflecting off of something on that man's chest."

"Only one thing reflects the sun like that off a man's chest," Gillett said. "A badge."

"Let's not get too excited," Clint said. "We don't want to shoot a deputy."

"How likely do you think it is that the sheriff we met has a deputy?" Gillett asked.

"Not very," Clint admitted, "but let's go slow anyway."

"What do you suggest?"

"Let's go and ask those two men if they know where the whorehouse is."

They walked toward the cantina as the two men stepped into the street. As they got closer, it became clear that the two men were Mexican. Closer still and Gillett saw what he had to see.

"That's my badge, Clint."

"Well," Clint said, "let's go get it back."

At the same time the two Mexicans saw the two men who were approaching them, and Pedro recognized one of them.

"*Hijo de un cabrón,*" he said under his breath.

"What?" José asked.

"That is the gringo Ranger we stole the badge from," Pedro said. "I told you that badge would get you in trouble—and me!"

"*Chinga tu madre!*" José shouted and went for his gun.

"Look out!" Clint shouted.

Gillett was on his left, so he pushed him away and went for his gun at the same time.

Just before the shooting started, Gillett yelled, "Don't plug my badge!"

He pulled the gun Clint had given him.

The man with the badge fired first, but too hurriedly. His shot went wild.

Clint fired next, and his bullet struck the man just below the badge. The force of the bullet staggered him backward. He tripped and went down on the boardwalk on his back.

The other Mexican fired next, but he had the same problem the first man had, he rushed his shot and missed cleanly.

Gillett fired the New Line and his bullet struck the man square in the center of the chest. He fired a second time because of the caliber of the gun, and the next bullet hit the man in the belly. He went down and was dead before he struck the dirt, face first.

Clint and Gillett moved forward cautiously to check the bodies.

"Dead," Clint said, standing over the man who was sprawled in the street.

"This one, too," Gillett said.

He bent over and removed his badge from the man's chest.

Clint looked around, but apparently shootings were not unusual in Socorro. No one seemed particularly interested in seeing what had happened, and the sheriff was nowhere in sight.

"How's the tin?" Clint asked.

"In one piece," Gillett said, "although your shot was pretty close. You almost took a piece off right at the bottom."

"What a complainer," Clint said.

Gillett laughed and pinned the badge on his own chest, where it belonged. He brushed off some imaginary spots with his sleeve and then turned so Clint could have a look.

"How's it look?" he asked.

Clint peered at it for a minute. Its shiny surface was spotless.

"Is that blood?" he asked, and then turned to walk away.

"Where?"

EIGHT

They recovered whatever money the two dead men had in their pockets. Gillett's gun they found in the saddlebags of one of the men. They were in the livery stable when the sheriff came by. He looked as if he had just awakened.

"Well," he said, "I guess you two made good your promise, huh?"

Clint and Gillett turned to look at the man.

"Well, well," Gillett said, "the local law is awake."

"Hey," the sheriff said, "everybody's gotta sleep, right? Even a Texas Ranger."

"Do you have some business with us, Sheriff?" Clint asked.

"I was just wonderin' if you were gonna be in town long enough to shoot anybody else."

Standing up, the sheriff didn't look any less disheveled. He was tall, though, over six feet, and very thin. He hadn't shaved in several days, apparently, and the growth on his face looked more like dirt than like a beard.

"What's your name, Sheriff?" Clint asked.

The sheriff frowned and asked, "Why?"

"I like to know who I'm talking to."

"Booth."

"Well, Sheriff Booth, we'll be in your town long enough to get one good night's sleep and then we'll be on our way. Is that all right with you?"

"That's fine with me, mister," the sheriff said. "I ain't lookin' for any more trouble in my town."

"Oh," Gillett said, "I'm sure you could handle just about anything that came along, Sheriff. Don't you think so, Clint?"

"Oh, sure," Clint said, "no problem. Of course, the trouble would have to be pretty loud, wouldn't it? I mean, after all, it would have to wake the sheriff up."

"Hey," the sheriff grumbled, "I'm just doin' my job, here."

"Well, Sheriff," Clint said, "maybe if you had done your job a little earlier two men wouldn't be dead, huh? What do you think of that?"

The sheriff scratched the growth on his face and said, "Naw. I think you boys would've killed them no matter what I done."

Clint and Gillett watched the man walk out.

"He might be right," Gillett said.

"You intended to kill them?" Clint asked.

"I don't think that matters," Gillett said. "They didn't give us much choice, did they?"

"No," Clint said, "I don't suppose they did."

"You want to get somethin' to eat?"

"Sounds like a good idea."

Gillett tossed his recovered saddlebags over his shoulder and said, "Let's go to the hotel so I can stow my gear, and then we can find someplace to eat. I hope there's a place with decent food."

"Or at least decent coffee," Clint said.

"Amen."

They found out that the cantina the two Mexicans had come out of that morning served food as well as whiskey and beer. From the hotel they walked over there, went inside, and sat at a table.

"*Señors*," the Mexican bartender said, "what can I get for you?"

"Something to eat," Gillett said.

"And coffee," Clint added.

"What have you got to eat?" Gillett asked.

"We have tortillas, enchiladas," the bartender said, "or I can make you each a nice steak."

"You got eggs?" Gillett asked.

"Oh, *sí, señor*, I have eggs."

"Good," Gillett said. "Steak and eggs for me, and coffee."

"I'll have the same," Clint said, "and bring the coffee right away, will you?"

"*Sí, señor*," the bartender said, almost snapping to attention. "*De inmediato!*"

True to his word, the bartender returned almost immediately with a pot of coffee and two cups.

"My wife, she is cooking your food," he said, "and my daughter will bring it out."

"Fine," Clint said.

As they sat there with their coffee, Gillett took out his gun and checked it for damage. First he ejected all the shells, and when he was finished examining the weapon he reloaded it and replaced it in his holster.

"What are your plans now?" Clint asked.

"The same as they were before," he said. "To find the Baca brothers."

"What if they doubled back on you?" Clint asked. "What if they're back in Texas?"

"That's not their pattern," Gillett said. "They generally come into Texas once a month. They've already been there this month."

"If you figure it that way," Clint said, "you've got until New Year's Eve to find them."

"I'll find them," Gillett said. "I'll give them a New Year's Eve to remember."

NINE

"So what's your plan, Jim?" Clint asked.

"What do you mean?" Gillett asked. "I just told you my plan."

"I mean, do you intend to kill the Baca boys or bring them back to Texas?"

"Well," Gillett said, "that's sort of their decision to make, isn't it?"

Clint thought a moment, thought about how the two Mexicans that morning had gone immediately for their guns. They had given Clint and Gillett no choice but to retaliate. That was probably what would happen with the Baca boys.

"I suppose it is, yeah."

"Naturally," Gillett said, "I'd prefer to take them back to Texas alive, but like I said, the choice is theirs. They do me more good alive than dead."

"How so?"

"I just want to ride them into Laredo and rub it in the face of my captain."

"Oh," Clint said, "I thought you were talking about a reward."

"Well," Gillett said, "there *is* a handsome reward on their heads, but as a Texas Ranger I can't collect it."

"I thought you were going after them unofficially," Clint said.

"I am," Gillett said, "but I'm still a Ranger. That doesn't change."

"Oh, I see."

A young Mexican woman came out of the kitchen then, carrying two plates. She was a pretty thing, about twenty-two, with bountiful breasts that were barely contained by the peasant blouse she was wearing. She was dark-haired and dark-eyed, and her skin was like cream. She gave Clint a saucy grin as she put his plate down in front of him and bumped his shoulder with her ample hip.

"Estralita!" her father shouted.

"*Sí, Papá?*"

"Go into the kitchen!"

"*Sí, Papá.*"

She gave Clint another look before scurrying into the kitchen.

"She likes you," Gillett said.

"Yeah," Clint said, "and I'll bet her papa has a big shotgun behind the bar."

They started to eat, and spent a few minutes in silence filling their empty bellies.

"You know," Gillett said, breaking the silence, "I

thought of something a little while ago."

"When?"

"When we were talking about a reward," Gillett said. "You could ride with me, help me catch them, and collect the reward yourself."

"Uh, I don't think so, Jim."

"There's five hundred dollars on each of their heads, Clint," Gillett said. "That would make for a nice Christmas, wouldn't it?"

Clint stopped and thought about a thousand dollars and how it would look in his bank account.

"I'm not a bounty hunter," he said, feeling uncomfortable.

"I know you're not," Gillett said, "but I could use somebody to watch my back, just in case I get careless again."

"That's true."

"And where's the harm in you collecting the money when we catch them?" Gillett said. "I'll do the dirty work, you just keep me alive until we catch them. See, you won't be hunting them, I will."

It was a fine line, Clint thought, but Christmas *was* coming, and a thousand dollars *was* a lot of money, and Gillett had already proven that he could be taken unawares. Clint liked Gillett and would hate to leave him and then hear later that he had gotten killed.

"All right," Clint said, "I'll come along to keep you company—and to keep you alive—but if we don't find them in the next five days, I'm heading for Texas. I want to be in Labyrinth for Christmas, and if I ride hard, I'll make it in two days."

"Okay," Gillett said, "agreed. Five days."

"When do you want to start?" Clint asked.

"Well, if you're only giving me five days, I want to start tomorrow."

"Are you feeling up to it?"

"Oh, yeah," Gillett said. "Getting my stuff back has made me feel a lot better. I still have a headache, but a good night's sleep ought to take care of that."

"All right, then," Clint said, "we'll start out at first light. What about supplies?"

"We'll travel light and pick up what we need along the way," Gillett said.

Clint knew that the Ranger didn't have much money, even after recovering what was left from the two Mexicans.

"I'll pick up some coffee and some bacon and beans," Clint said. "We can get by on that."

"Sounds good to me," Gillett said, "I'll want to check my horse over before we go, though. There's no telling what those two did to it."

"Good idea," Clint said. "You can do that after dinner so we don't have to do it in the morning."

Clint noticed that Gillett wasn't looking at him, or at his food. He turned his head to see what the other man *was* looking at and saw the bartender's daughter, Estralita. She was peering out at him from the kitchen, and when she saw him looking at her, she smiled.

"You have an admirer," Gillett said.

"Estralita!" her father called, and she ducked back into the kitchen.

"And she has a possessive father," Clint said. "That's the kind of trouble I don't need."

They finished their dinner and ordered more coffee,

which was brought by a contrite Estralita. She kept
her head and her eyes down, but she still took the
opportunity to bump his shoulder with her hip before
returning to the kitchen.

They finished the second pot of coffee and then Clint
paid the bill. The bartender stared hard at him while he
counted out the money.

"Boy," Gillett said, "there's one father I wouldn't want
to have mad at me."

"I didn't even do anything."

"Yeah," Gillett said, "yet."

As Clint and Gillett left the cantina two men across
the street watched them carefully. They watched to see if
the two men would walk together or split up. When they
did split up, the two men started after Gillett, hurrying
to keep him in sight.

TEN

While Gillett went to the livery to check on his horse, Clint went to the general store to buy the coffee, bacon, and beans. He took the supplies back to his hotel room with him and stuffed them into his saddlebags. If he had bought any more he would have needed a sack of some kind, but even though it was a tight fit, he got everything stowed away.

Gillett had given him back the Colt New Line, but instead of shoving it into the saddlebags with the supplies, he decided to wear it tomorrow. He'd tuck it into his belt at the small of his back. When you were hunting it never hurt to have a back-up gun.

After the supplies were stowed, he went to Gillett's door and knocked. When there was no answer, he assumed that the Ranger was still checking on his horse. He decided to walk over to the livery to check on Duke as well.

Gillett was bent over his horse, checking each hoof carefully, when he suddenly became aware of the fact that he wasn't alone. He stood up straight but did not turn around. He thought about it, but rejected it as a bad move.

"That's good," a man's voice said. "Just stand fast, don't make any sudden moves."

"Who are you?" Gillett asked.

"Just somebody who's been paid to kill you, Ranger," the voice said.

"By who?"

"You'd like to know, wouldn't you?"

"It would help."

"Believe me," the man said, "nothing is gonna help you now."

"You alone?"

"And if I am?" the man said. "Would that make you think about trying something?"

"Maybe."

"Well, there are two of us, but go ahead and try something," the man said. "You might as well die that way rather than taking one in the back."

"Don't be stupid," another voice said. "Plug him in the back."

"Yeah," Gillett said, "go ahead, shoot me in the back like the cowards you are."

"Hey," the second voice said, "watch it."

"Why?" Gillett said. "You gonna kill me even deader if I don't?"

"No," the second voice said, "but you could die a lot more painfully."

"What could be more painful than being shot in the back by a couple of cowards?"

"Why you—"

"Don't get too close," the first voice said. "That's what he wants you to do."

Too bad, Gillett thought, that one of them was smart enough to know that.

"Okay, come on, come on," Gillett said, "if you're gonna do it, do it, so I don't have to listen to the two of you anymore."

"Oh," the second voice said, "he's really asking for it."

"Okay, then," the first voice said, "let's get it over with."

Gillett heard the sound of two guns being cocked and knew he had to make a move now. . . .

Clint didn't encounter Gillett on the way to the livery, but he'd been in and out of the general store so fast that Gillett was probably still inside the stable. If he was going to check his horse over, he'd take his time doing it.

He reached the livery and heard voices inside. When he reached the doorway he saw two men holding guns. Gillett was not in sight, but he assumed that the Ranger was in the stall with his horse.

"Okay, then," one of the men said, "let's get it over with."

"Gillett!" Clint shouted and drew his gun.

His shout attracted the attention of both men, who turned his way. He shot one of them and then there was a shot from the stall and the other man fell.

Clint hurried in and kicked away the guns the two men had dropped. Gillett came out of his horse's stall, looking pale.

"Thanks," he said. "They got the drop on me."

"Are you always this careless?" Clint asked.

Instead of taking offense, Gillett scratched his head and answered the question seriously.

"I don't know," Gillett said. "Maybe I'm just getting old."

"You're younger than I am."

"Okay," Gillett said, "so I'm getting too old for this business."

He leaned over and checked both men to be sure they were dead, then went through their pockets.

"Did they say anything?" Clint asked.

"They said they were hired to kill me."

"Did they say by who?"

"No," Gillett said, looking up at Clint while he continued to rifle the dead men's pockets, "but it isn't hard to guess, is it?"

"The Bacas?"

"Who else? They know I'm on their trail, so they decided to take out a little insurance."

"Yeah," Clint said, "very little."

"Not so little," Gillett said, standing up. "If not for you, I'd be dead right now."

"Okay," Clint said, "so you had better insurance."

Gillett looked at Clint and said, "I sure did."

ELEVEN

Before they could turn in for the night, they had to go to the sheriff's office to talk to him.

"I thought you said you weren't gonna kill anybody else," the sheriff complained.

"What I meant was," Gillett said, "I wasn't going to kill anyone who wasn't trying to kill me first."

"Can't argue with that, can you, Sheriff?" Clint asked.

"No," the sheriff said, "I guess I can't. Do me a favor, though."

"What?"

"Leave town now?"

"We were planning to leave in the morning," Clint said, "and that's what we still aim to do."

"Do you think you can avoid killing anyone else?" the man asked.

"If nobody tries to kill us," Gillett said.

43

"Why don't you just go back to your hotel rooms and stay there?"

"You know something, Sheriff?" Clint said. "I think you came up with a good idea."

"A real surprise, huh?" Gillett asked.

The sheriff looked puzzled as they went out the door.

In front of the sheriff's office, Gillett said, "That actually is a good idea."

"I know," Clint said. "You can use the rest."

"You said it," Gillett said. "Maybe in the morning I'll be a little more alert."

As they walked back to the hotel, Clint thought, I hope so.

Gillett had been ambushed twice in the past twenty-four hours. If he made a habit of that, then Clint was going to be real busy trying to keep him alive. Then again, maybe the second time somebody got the drop on him was a result of the head injury from the first time.

Ah well, he guessed it was just a matter of time before he found out. At least the Ranger had reacted well in the livery. Maybe in the morning he'd be rested and in better shape. Clint hoped so, because his life was going to depend on Gillett just as much as the Ranger's was going to depend on him.

He decided that, come morning, if he wasn't confident that the Ranger was as healthy as he could be, he wouldn't go with him on his hunt. In fact, he'd try to talk the man out of it altogether, at least until he had shaken off the effects of his head injury.

• • •

Clint walked Gillett to his room and looked into the man's eyes before he went inside. What he saw convinced him that Gillett was not only tired, but *was* suffering from the effects of the bump on his head.

"Get a good night's sleep, Jim," Clint said. "I'll see you in the morning."

"Okay," Gillett said. "The way I feel, I might over-sleep, so don't be afraid to pound on the door and wake me up."

"Don't worry," Clint said. "I won't."

"Night, then."

"Good night."

Gillett started to go inside, then stopped and said, "Clint . . ."

Clint had started for his door, and he turned around at the sound of his name.

"Yes?"

"I don't know how to say this. . . . Uh, thanks," Gillett said.

"For what?"

"You saved my life twice now," Gillett said. "I owe you big."

"I'll collect big," Clint said. "Don't worry."

TWELVE

Clint removed both guns, setting the New Line on the table next to the bed and hanging his holster on the bedpost. He removed his boots and his shirt and lay on the bed with his hands behind his head. This was a lot earlier than he turned in when he was in most towns, but he thought it was a good idea. He had the room right next to Gillett's and he'd be able to hear if anything else happened. Who knew just how much insurance the Baca boys might have taken out? This way he'd be around if some more hired guns showed up.

Right then there was a knock on his door. He got up, wondering if it was Gillett. Maybe he couldn't sleep and was bored. That would make two of them. Maybe they should have got a bottle of whiskey and drank it and talked until they got sleepy.

He opened the door, but instead of James Gillett he saw the girl from the cantina, Estralita.

"Surprised?" she asked.

"Yes," he said. "What are you doing here?"

"You do not know?"

"Estralita—"

"Oooh," she said, hugging herself so that her breasts threatened to flow out of her blouse, "I like the way you say my name, *señor*. What is your name?"

"My name is Clint Adams," he said, "and you shouldn't be here."

"Why not?"

"Because you're very young."

"I am not so young as you think," she said.

"I think you're damned young."

"I am a woman," she said, "not a girl." She rocked from side to side and added, "Let me in and I will prove it to you."

"Estralita—"

"Then I will prove it to you here in the hall," she said, pouting. Suddenly, she hooked her thumbs into the bodice of her blouse and pulled it down so that her breasts bobbed free—and bob they did. She was very full-breasted for a girl—or woman—so short, and her nipples were large and brown.

"See?"

"Get in here before someone sees you," he said, pulling her inside and closing the door.

It was only later that he realized that was his undoing.

Much later. . . .

She woke him later in the night by putting her mouth to his ear and whispering, "Again, Clint?"

"Estralita," he said, "not all of us in this bed are as young as you are."

She giggled and slid her hand down his belly until she was holding his penis. Immediately, it began to swell in her hand.

"Ah," she said, "I see some parts of you are younger than others."

He moaned and said, "Some parts of me just have a mind of their own, that's all."

"Mmmm," she said, "the best parts, too."

She slithered down his body and began to pepper his young part with kisses.

"Jesus . . ." he groaned as she cupped his balls in one hand and wrapped her other hand around the base of his now erect penis. Suddenly, he was in her hot mouth and she was sucking him. He reached down to cup her head, which was bobbing up and down with increased speed. She moaned, and when he couldn't take it anymore he pulled her from him.

"Wait, wait, wait . . ." he said.

"Now you are awake, huh?" she asked, smiling and licking her lips. "Here, this will waken you even more." She turned in the bed, got on all fours, and presented him with her wonderfully full butt.

Fully awake, he got on his knees behind her, spread her legs, and poked between them with his penis. He found her hot, wet, and waiting, and pushed deeply into her from behind.

"*Aiee, Dios!*" she moaned. "You are in me so deep, Clint!"

He grasped her hips firmly and began to drive into her so that she couldn't talk. All she could do was grunt and gasp and moan.

"Oooh, oh, uhh," was mixed with an occasional, "Oh, yes," until suddenly he felt as if his whole body was exploding. . . .

Later still he woke to find her astride him, her full breasts dangling in his face. In fact, she had been brushing them across his lips and her nipples were fully erect.

"I know," he said, "you were sent here to try and kill me."

"Ah," she said, as he took one hard nipple into his mouth and slid deeply inside of her, "but what a wonderful way to die. . . ."

THIRTEEN

When Clint awoke the next morning, Estralita was lying on his outstretched left arm. He tried to slide it out from beneath her without waking her, and he'd almost succeeded when she stirred.

"Good morning," she said, smiling at him.

"Good morning."

"Mmmm," she said, stretching. The sheet fell away from her, and he had a clear view of her large breasts and brown nipples, her rounded belly, and full hips and thighs. He felt himself stirring. She was so young and full-bodied. As she got older she'd probably put on weight, but right now she was any man's dream of what a woman should look like in bed.

She saw his penis swelling and said, "*Dios mío*, you are not finished yet?"

He looked down at himself and said, "I guess not."

"You are much man, *señor*," she said, turning toward

him. She pressed her body to him and added, *"Muy hombre."*

"Too much man for you, Estralita?" he asked.

"Oh, no, *señor*," she said, pouting. "I do not think so." She bit his shoulder and then lifted his hand and placed it on her right breast. "But perhaps we should find out?"

While they dressed, Clint asked her, "Where does your father think you are, Estralita?"

"I do not know, *Señor* Clint," she said, adjusting her blouse.

"Do you disappear on him often?"

"Oh, no, Clint," she said, "only when a man such as you comes to town."

"And how many men such as me have you known before?" he asked.

"Such as *you*, *Señor* Clint?" she asked, all wide-eyed. "Why . . . none!"

He smiled at her and said, "Good answer."

Estralita left first, after she asked if he would be in town much longer.

"As a matter of fact," he answered, "I'll be leaving today."

"Oh," she said, "if I had known that, I would not have allowed you to waste so much time sleeping."

"Oh?" he said. "Did I sleep? I don't seem to remember that."

She laughed, kissed him good-bye, and left the room. He waited a few moments, then went down the hall to Gillett's room and knocked on the door.

He thought he was going to have to pound on it after all when suddenly it opened and Gillett was standing there, looking refreshed.

"Good morning," he said.

"Morning, Jim," Clint said. "How do you feel this morning?"

"I feel great," Gillett said. "I told you all I needed was a good night's sleep."

Clint looked into the man's eyes and saw that he was telling the truth. He did look alert and refreshed.

"And how did *you* sleep?" Gillett asked. The look on his face indicated he knew Clint had had company last night.

"Were you listening at the door?"

"I didn't have to listen at the door," Gillett said. "I could hear you through the walls. I assume it was little Estralita?"

"It was Estralita," Clint said, "and she's not so little."

"I'll bet," Gillett said. "Do we have time for some breakfast, or do we want to leave before her father comes looking for you?"

"If we can find someplace open for breakfast," Clint said, "I think we can chance it."

"All right, then," Gillett said, "let's go have a look. We might end up at the cantina, though. Think Estralita is in any shape to serve us—or is she all served out after last night?"

"Oh, shut up."

FOURTEEN

Enofre Baca—the eldest Baca brother—stared a-
cross the table at his younger brother, Abran.

"What are you lookin' at?" Abran demanded.

"You."

"Why?"

"I just want to see if you look as stupid as you are,"
Enofre said.

"What is so stupid, Enofre?"

"Wanting to go back to *Estados Unidos* so soon after
the last time," Enofre said. "That is what is stupid."

"Bah . . ." Abran said.

They both applied themselves to their breakfast after
that, involved with their own thoughts.

Enofre was thinking about the Texas Ranger who was
hunting them. First, he wondered *why* the man was so
intent on catching them. What had they done to him?
Second, he wondered whether the man was alive or
dead, if the two men they had paid to kill him had

been able to get the job done. Probably not. They did not seem very competent.

Abran was thinking about the Texas Ranger, too. He didn't think the two men they hired would be good enough to kill him. Abran chose to think that the man was still on their trail, and the only way he could think of to get him off their trail—other than killing him themselves—was to double back to Texas again. The Ranger would not expect them to do that. But he could not get his brother to realize that. His brother had a head like stone. *Cabeza de Piedra!*

"Head like stone," he said aloud.

"What?"

"I was just thinkin' that you have a head like stone," Abran said.

"Abran," Enofre said, "you must speak to me with respect. I am the older brother."

"You are the more *stubborn* brother, that is for sure," Abran said.

Enofre put his fork down and stared across the table at his brother.

"It is foolhardy to go back to Texas so soon," he said. "In fact, it might be foolish to *ever* go back to Texas."

"What would you suggest we do?"

"I think we should go back home to Ol' Mexico," Enofre said.

"And then what do we do when we . . . get the urge?" the younger brother asked.

Enofre grinned and said, "We ride into New Mexico? Then we would not have the Texas Rangers to deal with."

"We do not have the Texas *Rangers* to deal with, *mi hermano*, we have *one* Texas Ranger to deal with. I wish I knew *why* he wanted to catch us so badly."

Enofre shrugged and said, "Perhaps he simply feels that it is his job."

"Bah," Abran said, "I have never known a man so dedicated to his job, before. Perhaps we should simply wait for him and ask him why he hunts us with such . . . vigor!"

"And then what?"

"And then we kill him."

Enofre, who as the older brother felt that he was also the leader, said, "I will think about your suggestion, Abran."

"You do that, Enofre," Abran said, shaking his head helplessly.

Abran, although he was younger, knew that he was the smarter brother. Of course, he did not tell Enofre this. He allowed Enofre to think that he made all the decisions, when in reality it was he, Abran, who made them. If not for Abran, they would not have known how to satisfy these urges that came over them. Enofre would have been content to kick a dog or rape a woman during the urge, but it was Abran who realized that there were more satisfying ways of getting their . . . relief.

So Enofre could do all the thinking he wanted to do. It would not matter. They would do what Abran decided—even if he had to make Enofre think that it was *his* decision.

FIFTEEN

As it turned out, there was not a place open that early for breakfast—not even the cantina, which was just as well as far as Clint was concerned. He'd just as soon not have to face Estralita's father.

Giving up on breakfast, they went to the hotel, collected their gear, checked out, and walked to the livery to saddle their horses. The liveryman offered to saddle the animals for them, but both Clint and Gillett preferred to do it themselves.

"I hope my gray can keep up with your gelding," Gillett said.

"He looks healthy," Clint said. "Besides, we're not going to push it, are we?"

"I don't think so."

"I assume you tracked the Baca boys this far before you were ambushed."

"I did," Gillett said.

"Where do you figure they'll head from here?" Clint asked.

"South is all I figure," Gillett said. "I think they'd want to put as much space between them and Texas as they could, until the next time."

"Maybe we'll get lucky," Clint said, "and meet them on the way back."

"That *would* be lucky."

"Guess we can't count on that."

"I've never relied on luck much," Gillett said, "and I don't think you have, either."

"No."

"Although," Gillett said, turning to face Clint, "I was pretty lucky that it was you who came along and found me lying on the ground."

"Don't start thanking me again, Gillett," Clint said. "It's getting tiresome."

"Okay, okay," Gillett said, "no more thank-you's."

They walked their horses outside and mounted up there.

"You know," Clint said, "we never did ask the sheriff if he saw the Baca brothers."

"He said he didn't see any strangers."

"Yeah," Clint said, "but maybe they aren't strangers to him."

"Maybe not," Gillett said thoughtfully. "Maybe we should go ask him before we leave."

When they entered the sheriff's office they heard the snoring once again. This time they did not hesitate. They went right to the cell and shook him awake. They also did not allow him to simply lie there and talk to them. They shook him hard enough so that he had to sit up to avoid falling off the pallet he was sleeping on.

"What the hell—"

"We're leaving town, Sheriff," Clint said.

The man rubbed his eyes and stared up at them.

"You woke me up to tell me that?"

"No," Gillett said, "we woke you up to ask you when was the last time you saw the Baca brothers?"

The sheriff hesitated, then said, "Uh, who?"

"Don't play games, Sheriff," Gillett said. "We're talking about the Baca boys. They're cold-blooded killers, and you're a lawman. Remember that. Now, when was the last time you saw them?"

"Uh . . . three, maybe four days ago."

"Shit," Gillett said. He had been two days behind them, and now he was four days behind them. "We'll have to catch up," he said to Clint.

"We will."

"There's something you should know," the sheriff said.

"What?"

"They have a gang."

"Do they?" Clint asked.

"How many?" Gillett said.

"I'm not sure," the sheriff said. "I've just . . . heard."

Gillett stared at the man, then said, "Thanks, Sheriff. You can go back to sleep now."

They left the man sitting up, still trying to blink sleep from his eyes.

Outside Gillett said, "What do you think?"

"About the gang?"

"Yeah."

"I think it would be nice if we could catch these brothers before they join up with their gang."

"If there is a gang."

"Why would he say there was if there wasn't?" Clint asked.

"I don't know."

"Has there ever been a report of them riding with a gang in Texas?"

"No," Gillett said, "not that I've ever heard."

"Well," Clint said, "I guess we'll find out soon enough, won't we?"

As they mounted up, Gillett said, "Well, this seems to be another piece of luck."

"What?"

"Having you along," the Ranger said. "I mean, if we run into them and they have a gang with them . . . It might have been, um, inconvenient if I ran into them alone."

"Yeah," Clint said, "inconvenient. That's a nice way to put it."

"At least now there's two of us."

"And how many of them?" Clint asked. Neither of them had an answer, though.

They'd have to find that out the hard way.

SIXTEEN

They rode all day without stopping so that they were pretty tired when they finally did stop for the night.

"How are you holding up?" Clint had asked at one point.

"I'm fine," Gillett had said, almost annoyed. "Don't be like a mother hen."

"Okay," Clint said. From then on, he just kept an eye on the Ranger, but he never asked him how he was feeling.

When they stopped to camp, they divvied up the chores. Gillett collected wood for the fire while Clint took care of the horses. By the time Clint had the animals taken care of, Gillett had the fire going. Clint took the coffee and food from the saddlebags and put them on the fire.

The coffee was ready first, and they each had a cup while they waited for the bacon and beans.

"I'm going to get tired of bacon and beans pretty quick," Clint said.

"It's better than nothing," Gillett said.

"You know," Clint said, "I never did ask you what your rank in the Rangers is."

"Oh," Gillett said, "I'm a sergeant."

Clint heard a note of disdain in Gillett's voice.

"It doesn't seem to mean much to you," he said.

"It doesn't," Gillett said. "I just want to do my job, that's all. My rank doesn't matter much—that is, unless they make me a captain."

"And then what?"

"Then I resign."

"Why?"

"Because the last thing I want to do is sit behind some goddamn desk," Gillett said, "which is what a captain does. He sits on his butt and sends his men out to get shot at."

"Somebody has to make the decisions, I guess," Clint said.

Gillett did not reply.

When the bacon and beans were ready, Clint dished them out and handed Gillett a plate.

"How long have you been with the Rangers?" he asked.

"About five years."

"What did you do before that?"

"This and that," Gillett said. "I was a lawman, a bounty hunter, a ranch hand. Let's see . . . I was a bartender, a bouncer . . . oh, I dealt blackjack for a while."

"Sounds like you did a lot of different things," Clint said.

"I'll bet you did, too."

"Oh, I was a lawman, and I've dealt some poker. I even tended some bar . . . oh yeah, and I hunted some buffalo."

"See? We're not so different—except that you were never a bounty hunter."

"I don't have anything against it," Clint said. "It's just not anything I ever wanted to do."

"And I never hunted buffalo," Gillett said. "I think that's something I would have liked to do. I guess there aren't many of them left, huh?"

"No," Clint said. "It's a shame. I'll tell you, a herd of buffalo was a beautiful sight, especially if they were on the run."

"I can imagine," Gillett said. "At least I think I can."

After dinner they cleaned up, and Clint made another pot of coffee.

"Okay," Gillett said, "this time we'll share the watch, four hours on and four hours off."

"No argument from me," Clint said. "I'm going to sleep like a baby until you wake me."

"Wait a minute," Gillett said. "Who says I get the first watch?"

"Okay, fine," Clint said, "I'll take the first watch, then."

"Well . . . why should you take the first watch?" the Ranger asked.

"*Somebody's* got to take the first watch, right?" Clint said.

"Okay, then," Gillett said, "*I'll* take the first watch."

"What a good idea," Clint said, "and I'll sleep like a baby until you wake me up."

Gillett frowned and asked, "Why do I feel like I just lost something?"

The first watch went without incident. Before waking Clint, though, Gillett made a fresh pot of coffee.

"Clint," he said, softly at first. He meant to raise his voice the second time, but the second time wasn't necessary.

"I'm awake," Clint said from beneath his blanket. "It was the smell of the coffee that did it."

"Here," Gillett said, handing him a cup.

"Thanks."

"Everything's quiet," Gillett said, settling down on the ground and pulling his blanket around him.

Clint stood up, holding the coffee cup with one hand and keeping the blanket around him with the other. He watched the vapor come from his mouth as he breathed.

"Jesus, it's cold," he said.

"Tell me about it," Gillett said from inside his blanket. "Wake me when the sun comes up and we'll get an early start."

"Damn," Clint muttered, "I'd rather start now. It'd be better to be moving in this cold than staying still."

Gillett didn't answer. He was already asleep.

SEVENTEEN

When Enofre and Abran Baca rode into the town of Never Bend, New Mexico, they each had the same thing in mind—women.

When "the urge" started to come over them, being with a woman usually satisfied it, at first. It was when it grew more intense that even stronger *methods* were needed.

As they were approaching Never Bend, Abran started to feel it, and he knew that if he was feeling it, his brother was feeling it, too, for Enofre and Abran were twins. When one felt something, usually the other felt it, as well.

Enofre—the eldest by three minutes—fidgeted in his saddle, which was how Abran knew that his brother was feeling the same thing. Enofre generally reacted to the urge by becoming fidgety and nervous, while Abran reacted by withdrawing into himself.

They left their horses at the livery and went to the hotel.

"Where's the whorehouse?" Abran asked the desk clerk after they had checked in.

"What?" The clerk was a small man, fussily dressed and obviously nervous in their presence.

"The whores," Enofre said. "Where will we find the whores?"

"You would not have any use for a woman," Abran said to the clerk, "but we do."

"A use," Enofre said, "and a need."

Abran gave his brother a warning look.

"Just tell us where we can find some women," Abran said to the man.

"Uh," the man said, "you can go to the saloon—"

"Not saloon girls," Abran said. "Whores!" He almost shouted the word, leaning across the desk.

"The end of the street," the clerk said quickly. "Miss Abigail's."

"Abigail?" Enofre said, wrinkling his nose. "I hope her whores are prettier than her name."

"A gringo name," Abran said.

They went to their room to dump their belongings, then left the hotel in search of Miss Abigail's.

Abigail Carter turned out to be a woman in her fifties. Obviously, she was an ex-whore who had gone to fat and become a madam.

"You boys just ride into town?" she asked.

"That is right."

"And you're hungry, huh?" she asked. "For some female companionship?"

"That's right," Enofre said. "Hungry."

"Do you have money? Eh?" Abigail asked.

"Don't worry," Abran said. "We have money."

"Well . . . all right, then," Abigail said. She had intended to ask them for the money in advance, but she was intimidated by them. In fact, they scared her. "I have just the girls for you."

"We will pick the girls ourselves," Abran said.

Abigail's intention had been to give them to Wendy and Gloria. They were her most experienced girls, used to handling almost any kind of man.

"Well . . . all right, then," she said. "Come into the sitting room and take your pick."

She took the two Mexicans into the sitting room, where girls were sitting around on overstuffed divans, in different stages of dress—and undress.

"I want that one," Enofre said immediately.

The girl he picked was a young blonde named Patsy. Abigail flinched, because Patsy, at nineteen, was her newest girl.

"She's new," Abigail said. "I can give you someone with more experience—"

Enofre turned and glared at the madam and said, "I want her."

"And I want her," Abran said.

At Abran's choice, Abigail heaved a sigh of relief. He had picked the dark-haired Wendy, who was thirty-four and her *most* experienced girl.

"Well, all right, gents," Abigail said, maintaining her professional demeanor. "Ladies, these gentlemen would like your company upstairs."

The two women got up, walked over to the Baca

brothers, and took them by the arm. On their faces were the smiles they had learned to wear, no matter what the men they were with looked like.

"'You treat them good," Abigail said, which is what she usually told her girls when they were going upstairs. This time, however, she felt she was speaking to the men as well as the women—maybe even more so.

"Treat them *real* good," she said under her breath as the two couples disappeared up the stairs.

When Abran entered the room with Wendy, she said, "How would you like it, mister?"

"Rough," he said.

She put her hands on her hips and said, "I can handle it rough. Do you want me to be rough with you, or you with me?"

"Get undressed," he said.

"Sure."

She was only wearing a filmy nightgown over black underwear, and she discarded all of it and stood before him for his inspection.

She was a solidly built woman, full in the breasts and the hips as well as in the butt. Her legs were powerful, heavy in the thighs and muscular in the calves. She had the darkest nipples he had ever seen, and that excited him.

Abran liked the way she looked. He had learned that more fragile women could not stand up to the treatment he gave them.

Unfortunately, Enofre had not yet learned that lesson.

•　•　•

Patsy stood naked in front of Enofre, who drank in the sight of her. She was slightly built, with small, rounded breasts, a tiny waist, and slender hips. She was nervous, but Enofre did not notice this.

He undressed, and her eyes widened when his hardening penis came into view. He was the biggest man she had ever seen down there, and now she was worried that she might not be able to accommodate him.

"Don't worry about size, honey," Abigail had told her once during her lessons, "it stretches."

Staring at Enofre, Patsy hoped that it would stretch *that* much.

EIGHTEEN

An hour later a girl named Lisa burst into the sheriff's office.

"Sheriff," she said breathlessly, "I think you better come quick."

"What's the matter, girl?" Sheriff Horace Golding asked her.

"He's killin' her, Sheriff," she said anxiously. Her eyes were so wide, he could see white all the way around her pupils. "Miss Abigail sent me to get you because he's killin' her!"

"Jesus," Golding said, and came out of his chair as fast as his two hundred and fifty pounds of fat would allow.

"Open this door, damn it!" Abigail shouted, pounding on the door to Patsy's room.

From inside they could still hear Patsy screaming, though her cries were becoming weaker and weaker.

69

"He's killing her, Abigail," one of the girls said, crying.

"I know that!" Abigail shouted. She looked up and down the hall and saw only her girls.

"Where the hell is Luthor?" she shouted.

"I'm coming!" a man's voice shouted.

With that a big, black man bounded into view from the staircase, holding in his hand a big wooden club.

"Open this door, Luthor," Abigail shouted. "Now!"

From his room Abran could hear the racket going on in the hall.

Wendy was beneath him, staring up at him sightlessly. His huge member was buried inside of her, and she had bite marks on her neck and breasts. Unlike his brother, Abran had not allowed *his* woman to shout. He had kept one hand over her mouth and the other around her neck until she stopped struggling, and then had proceeded to ravage her with his teeth, and his penis.

He pounded into her until his release came, and even then he did not allow *himself* to shout, even though he wanted to.

Now that he was done with her, he got off of her, off of the bed, and hurriedly got dressed. Before leaving the room, he wiped his mouth on the sheet.

Enofre was going to need help . . . again.

"Stand back, girls," the big man hollered.

The girls moved away. Luthor braced himself against the opposite wall and then ran forward, striking the door with his shoulder.

As it slammed open, Abigail realized that Patsy had stopped screaming.

She rushed into the room behind Luthor, who had stopped short at what he saw on the bed.

Enofre was on the bed, straddling Patsy, whose torso was a mass of blood. When the Mexican turned his head to see what the intrusion was about, they could see that his mouth was covered with blood. It was then that Abigail knew that the wounds on Patsy had been inflicted by the man's teeth.

"My God!" she said. "Luthor!"

"Mister," Luthor said, lifting his club, "you is a dead man."

Enofre looked over at his gun, which he had left too far from the bed to get to. He looked back at Luthor and the club that would soon descend on him.

There was a shot then, and Abigail saw a hole appear in Luthor's back. A second shot came, and a second bloody hole bloomed, and Luthor fell to the floor.

"Come on, Enofre!" Abran called from the door. "Time to go."

Abran was cursing inside. The urge had gotten the best of both of them, but at least he had been quiet about it. If Enofre had done the same, they could have left, checked out of the hotel, and collected their horses before anyone was the wiser. Now getting out of town was going to be messy.

Also, this was the first time that the urge had gotten the better of them in New Mexico. They were usually able to hold out until they got to Texas. Now they really were going to have to head for Ol' Mexico.

• • •

As Sheriff Golding entered Miss Abigail's, he heard the screaming from upstairs and it made his blood run cold. In the past he knew that cowboys would get out of hand and beat one of the girls up. It had happened plenty of times before, but this time the screams he heard had an edge of panic to them.

Jesus, he thought as he ran up the stairs with his gun in his hand, what the hell was happening up there?

He never made it to the top of the stairs.

Two men appeared above him on the landing, one of them with bloodstains on his face. Golding stopped short, and the two men both lifted their guns and fired at the same time.

NINETEEN

"You know," Clint said, on the fourth night that they camped, "you never did tell me exactly what these Baca brothers do."

"You never asked."

"Well, I'm asking now," Clint said. "I know you said they were killers, but who have they killed?"

Gillett took the time to pour himself another cup of coffee before answering. When he did, he had a look on his face that was as cold as stone.

"They kill women," he said. "They rape them, and brutalize them, and leave them dead."

"Jesus."

"They've done it to whores," Gillett said, "but when there's no whore around they just . . . choose any girl. Usually, they each take a girl, and both girls end up being dead."

"How do they do it?"

Gillett shook his head and said, "I've never seen

anything like it. They usually kill the women by strangling them, or smothering them somehow—in one case they broke a girl's neck. But it's . . . what else they do that's so horrible."

Clint decided to wait and let Gillett tell it in his own time.

"They . . . *bite* them."

"They what?"

"They take huge chunks out of their flesh with their teeth," Gillett said. "They're like . . . ferocious animals, like dogs or wolves who use their teeth on their victims, tearing pieces from them."

Clint hesitated and then said, "You've actually seen this, Jim?"

"Oh, I've seen it," Gillett said. "I've seen some of the women afterward, Clint. They're . . . ravaged! Covered with blood. And I've heard reports of the Baca boys running from the scene with . . . blood all over their mouths and faces."

"Jesus Christ," Clint said under his breath. "No wonder you want them so bad."

"Yeah," Gillett said, "I want them bad. You know, I've hunted—and caught—all kinds of two-legged varmints—and vermin. These two, though, they're the worst."

"I wonder about their gang," Clint said.

"If they're as bad, you mean?"

"No," Clint said, "if they know what kind of men the Bacas are. You know, most men—even outlaws—don't hold with brutalizing women."

"You're right," Gillett said. "That might come in handy if we run into the whole gang at the same time."

"We'll have to keep that in mind."

• • •

The Bacas put some distance between them and Never Bend before they stopped to camp for the night. They stopped right by a water hole.

"Wash that blood off your face!" Abran told his brother.

Enofre went to the water hole and washed his face. When he returned, his brother had a fire going.

"Take care of the horses," Abran said.

"Why didn't you—"

"Because I built the fire."

"Well, who says that *you* say who does what—" Enofre started, but Abran cut him off before he could get much further.

"Look!" he said, standing up and facing his older brother. "You almost got us into trouble in Never Bend, Enofre. When are you gonna learn *not* to let your women scream?"

Enofre's eyes glazed over as he thought back and he said, "I like when they scream, Abran. It . . . satisfies the urge more, you know?"

Abran did know. He knew that his brother was a sick man who liked to make women scream. Abran didn't like the screaming. It hurt his ears and took away his concentration. It kept him from enjoying what really mattered.

"I don't know what I'm going to do with you, Enofre," Abran said.

"What are we going to do now?" Enofre asked. "You still want to go back to Texas?"

"No," Abran said, "I think now that you had the right idea."

"Ol' Mexico?"

"Yes," Abran said. "We can't stay in New Mexico anymore. They'll be looking for us."

"Especially after we killed that fat sheriff," Enofre said.

"Yes," Abran said, "that, too."

Enofre started to laugh.

"What are you laughing at?" Abran asked.

"That fat sheriff," Enofre said, giggling. "I'm surprised the bullets went through the fat."

As Enofre continued to laugh, Abran looked at his brother and said, "You are a sick man, Enofre. A very sick man."

TWENTY

When Clint and Gillett rode into Never Bend, they both had the feeling they had missed something. It was a sixth sense that they had each developed over the years, and they had come to trust it.

"Something happened here recently," Clint said.

"I feel it, too."

"Like a shadow over the whole town."

"Yup."

Clint looked at Gillett and said, "The sheriff's office?"

"Yup," Gillett said again.

They rode up to the sheriff's office and dismounted. When they tried the door, though, it was locked.

"They lock the door to the sheriff's office?" Gillett asked.

"I don't like this," Clint said, looking around. "It's midday, it's not like he didn't come to work yet."

"Maybe he's asleep in one of the cells," Gillett suggested.

Clint pounded on the door for a while, but to no avail. No one answered.

"Let's go over to the livery," he said. "We can put the horses up and maybe the liveryman will know what's going on."

"Could be it's just a quiet town," Gillett said.

"Could be," Clint said, "but I doubt it."

"He's dead?" Clint said to the liveryman.

"That's right," the man said. He spit some tobacco and then added, "Shot dead three days ago."

"Three days," Gillett said. "Who shot him?"

"Coupla Mex's."

"Mexicans?" Gillett said.

"That's what I said."

"What happened?"

"It happened over at Miss Abigail's," the liveryman said.

"What's Miss Abigail's?" Clint asked. "The local, uh, entertainment?"

"If ya like women it is, yup," the man said. "Seems like these two Mex's got rough with a coupla the girls. They sent for the sheriff, and he got shot dead."

"What happened to the girls?" Gillett asked.

"Don't rightly know," the man said. "Guess you'd have to ask Miss Abigail."

"I guess we will," Clint said. "Thanks. How do we get to Miss Abigail's?"

"Are you the law?" Abigail Carter asked.

"I'm a Texas Ranger, ma'am," Gillett said.

"What are you doing in New Mexico?"

"I'm hunting a couple of Mexican outlaws," he said. "Killers, really. I heard there was some trouble here a few days ago?"

She had kept them standing on the doorstep, but now she backed up and allowed them to enter.

"Come in," she said.

She led them to the sitting room, where some of the girls were. It was too early for them to be dressed for work, so most of them were pretty much covered up. Still, Clint couldn't help noticing that some of them were very pretty.

"Yeah, I guess you could say we had some trouble," Abigail said.

"What kind of trouble, ma'am?" Gillett asked. "We heard the sheriff got killed."

"He did," she said, "but that's actually the least of it."

"Would you like to tell us about it?" Clint asked.

"Why not?" she said. "Nobody's been doing anything about it so far. Maybe you will."

She told them about the two Mexicans who came to be with a couple of the girls.

"I knew they were bad as soon as I saw them, but what can I do? I run a business, and most folks who come here ain't exactly saints."

"We understand."

"They went upstairs, and the next thing I know little Patsy's screaming her head off. We ran up there and I tried to get the door open, but I couldn't. Meanwhile, Patsy's screamin' like he's killin' her, so I sent Lisa for the sheriff."

One of the girls looked up, and Clint figured she was Lisa. She was dark-haired with a wide mouth and slightly prominent teeth. Some men might have called her horse-faced, but then some men liked women with wide mouths. She was actually quite attractive.

"Well, Patsy kept screamin' and I kept poundin' on the door until Luthor finally showed up."

"Who's Luthor?" Gillett asked.

"He's the black man I kept here as a bouncer," she said. "He kicked the door in and by this time Patsy had stopped screamin'. When we got inside we saw why. He'd killed her."

"How?" Gillett asked.

"Well, the doctor said she was strangled, but . . . but that . . . monster had taken bites out of her. I mean he . . . he took *pieces* out of her. He had blood all over his mouth!"

"Take it easy," Gillett said. "What else happened?"

"Well, it happened real fast after that," she said, with her hands over her mouth. "The other Mexican came out of nowhere and shot poor Luthor in the back. When they started to leave, the sheriff showed up. He was comin' up the stairs and they both shot him. After that they just took off."

"And left town?"

"That's right," she said. "After they left, we discovered poor Wendy."

"Wendy?"

"She went into her room with the other Mexican, and he killed *her*."

"Did he . . . abuse her the same way?"

"Yeah," she said, "but it wasn't as bad as the other one. He was like a . . . a wild *animal*!"

Gillett looked at Clint and said, "It was them."

"The men you're lookin' for?" Abigail asked.

"That's right."

"Will you keep lookin' for them?"

"Oh, yes, ma'am," Gillett said. "I'll keep looking for them just as long as it takes me to find them. I can promise you that."

"Then promise me somethin' else, Ranger."

"What's that, ma'am?"

"Promise me that you'll kill them when you find them," she said. "Can you do that?"

"I think I can safely say that I can, ma'am," Gillett said. "I surely can."

When they got outside Clint put his hand on Gillett's arm.

"Why did you do that?"

"Do what?"

"Why did you promise her that you'd kill them?" Clint demanded.

"Why?" Gillett said, staring at him. "Come with me, Clint."

"Where?"

"I want to show you something," Gillett said.

"What?"

"Just come with me, will you?" Gillett said. "Please?"

TWENTY-ONE

Clint wondered where Gillett was taking him, particularly since neither of them had ever been in Never Bend, New Mexico, before. Finally, Gillett had to stop someone to ask for directions and Clint knew where he was being taken.

The undertaker's.

"What do we want here, Jim?" Clint asked as they entered the undertaker's office.

"I want you to see them, Clint," Gillett said. "I want you to see what the Bacas do to women."

The undertaker came out, a small, potbellied man with a wispy white halo of hair.

"Can I help you gents?" he asked. "Have you suffered a loss?"

"Not recently," Gillett said. "I want to see the women who were killed a few days ago."

"Jim—" Clint said.

"Uh, mister—" the undertaker started.

"Look," Gillett said, "I just want my friend to see them, that's all. He asked me how I can promise to kill the men who did it. The only way I can explain it to him is to let him see the girls."

"Jim, listen—"

"Mister," the undertaker said, "them girls is buried already."

"What?" Gillett asked.

"That's what I was trying to tell you, Jim," Clint said. "They were killed three days ago. They're in the ground by now."

For a moment Gillett looked totally confused, and Clint realized that the Ranger had not yet fully recovered from his head injury. Either that, or he was just upset about the two women and was not thinking straight.

"Jim," Clint said, "come on, let's go get a drink."

"I don't . . ." Gillett started, then stopped.

"Jim."

"I don't know what I was thinking."

"You weren't thinking," Clint said. "That's okay. Come on, let's get a drink." Clint looked at the undertaker and said, "Sorry to have bothered you."

"That's all right," the undertaker said. He looked at Gillett and said, "I can tell your friend how they looked, if you like."

"Yes," Gillett said, "yes, tell him."

"Jim—" Clint said, trying to pull the man toward the door.

"No, wait," Gillett said, resisting. "I want you to hear this." He looked at the undertaker and asked, "What's your name, sir?"

"Tupper," the man said, "Austin Tupper, sir."

"Mr. Tupper," Gillett said, "tell my friend what those women looked like."

"Well, the older one, Wendy, she wasn't too bad," Tupper said. "She'd been strangled—both girls had— but Wendy had these bite marks on her body. On her neck and her . . . her breasts. The other one, though, the younger one . . . My God, she had beautiful skin, she did. . . ."

Clint stared at the man, who seemed to be looking inside his head at something only he could see—but he was describing it so Clint could see it, too—and Clint didn't like what he was seeing.

"That little one, she was bit up something awful. I mean, the man had taken *chunks* out of her with his teeth, awful bites, you know . . ."

"I know. . . ." Gillett said.

"Jesus," Clint said, grabbing Gillett's arm, "come on, Jim, now *I* need a drink."

TWENTY-TWO

They found a saloon, and Clint ordered a bottle of whiskey without even asking Gillett what he wanted. They took the bottle and two glasses to a table. Clint poured two drinks, and they each downed their shots quickly. He poured two more, but these they worked on slowly.

"What's going on, Jim?" Clint asked.

"What do you mean?"

"You're too . . . intense about this for it to just be your job," Clint said. "Your concentration is not there, you've been too careless, you're just not thinking straight."

"I'm just upset—"

"I know you are," Clint said, "but why?"

For a moment Clint wasn't sure Gillett was even listening to him, but then the man lifted his head and looked at him. There was a tortured look in his eyes that he hadn't seen before, and he realized that the

Ranger had probably been hiding it from him. Now it was naked and out in the open, and it was a terrible thing to see.

"You want to know what's going on?" Gillett asked. "Okay, I'll tell you. When the Bacas came to Laredo, they killed two women, two women who weren't whores. They just happened to be in the wrong place at the wrong time, and the Bacas grabbed them. They dragged them into an alley, and they beat them, and raped them, then they strangled them and . . . and did horrible things to them."

Clint continued to stare at Gillett. That was a terrible thing to hear, but he knew that couldn't be all of it. There was more to come.

"One of those women was my sister," Gillett said finally.

"Jesus," Clint said, suddenly understanding the man's anguish and his need to catch the two killers. "Jim, why didn't you tell me—"

"The other one," Gillett went on, "had she lived, would have become my wife."

Clint sat back in stunned silence.

"So that's what's going on," Gillett said. He lifted his drink, finished it, and poured another. His hand was shaking badly. "That's why I can't concentrate, that's why I've been careless. . . ."

"That's why your captain told you to stay out of it," Clint said. "Because you're too close, too involved."

"I'm the only one who wants them badly enough, Clint," Gillett said. "I'm the only one who wants them badly enough to follow them anywhere. Can you understand that?"

"Yes, I can."

"And can you understand why I can't just sit and wait for them to be caught?"

"Yes," Clint said, "I understand that, too, Jim. I understand it all, and I'm with you."

"I need you," Gillett said. "I need you *because* I'm too close, *because* my concentration is off. I need you to keep me from getting killed until I can kill them."

"I'm with you, Jim," Clint said. "Right up until we catch them."

Gillett looked at Clint and asked, "Even if it takes until after Christmas?"

"Even if it takes the rest of this year," Clint said, "and all of the next."

They each finished their drink, and Clint poured out two more.

"I'm obliged, Clint."

"Just tell me one thing."

"What?"

"Are you still a Texas Ranger?"

"I was when I left Laredo," Gillett said. "My captain— Edmonds is his name—he threatened to suspend me if I didn't stay out of it. Maybe he has, I don't know. All I know is I still have my badge. As far as I'm concerned, I'm still a Ranger."

"Okay," Clint said. "That's good enough for me."

Clint poured one more drink and then stoppered the bottle.

"What are you doing?" Gillett asked. It came out like an accusation. Clint hadn't yet seen Gillett drunk, although the man seemed to have every right to be. Still, he didn't think now would be the right time.

"No more."

"Why not?"

"Because we're riding out," Clint said, "and we don't want to fall off our horses."

"Riding out?"

Clint reached across the table and very deliberately took Gillett's glass from in front of him.

"There's no point in staying in town tonight, Jim," Clint said. He was speaking slowly, as if to a child. "We'll only fall further behind. We've made up a day on them, because they were here three days ago. If we keep riding, we'll make up even more time on them."

Gillett squinted at Clint, then sat back and vigorously rubbed his eyes.

"Okay," he said, "okay, so let's get going."

They stood up, left the half-finished bottle of whiskey on the table, and went to the livery stable to collect their horses.

TWENTY-THREE

By the time they camped that night, Gillett seemed to have collected himself.

"Sorry about this afternoon," he said when they were seated around the fire.

"Sorry for what?"

"I sort of came apart."

"Not that I've noticed," Clint said. "Now that I know what you're going through, I'm kind of surprised you didn't fall apart a long time ago."

"Oh," Gillett said, "I did my fair share of crying and wringing my hands back when it first happened."

"When was that?"

"A little over three weeks ago," Gillett said. "Actually, it's twenty-two days, today."

"You've been hunting the Bacas for twenty-two days?" Clint asked.

"No," Gillett said, "I spent six days crying, wringing my hands, feeling sorry for myself, drinking, arguing with my captain, and then finally got on their trail."

"That still comes out to sixteen days," Clint said. "And you started six days behind them."

"Yeah," Gillett said. "I narrowed it to two before the ambush."

"And then four," Clint said, "and now we're back to three. Tell me, since you've been on their trail for that long, what do you think they'll do now?"

"Actually," Gillett said, "I've been after them on and off for a few months, just as part of my job. They kept hitting and running, hitting and running, and then . . . well, they just hit too close to home."

"So now that they've killed here in New Mexico, what will they do? Double back and head for Texas again?"

"No," Gillett said, "they're wanted in Texas, and they'll be wanted in New Mexico now. My guess is they'll head for Mexico."

"And you'll go in after them?"

"Yes," Gillett said, pouring himself another cup of coffee. "You don't have to go with me if you don't want to, Clint."

"Hey," Clint said, "I don't have a problem with going to Mexico. I've been there before, I even have some friends there. Besides, I've never spent Christmas in Mexico. It might be interesting."

"This is the fifth day, you know," Gillett said.

"What fifth day?"

"The five days you told me you'd give me, remember?" Gillett asked. "This is the fifth one."

"Well," Clint said, "that's gone by the wayside, hasn't it? I'm committed to this thing now, Jim."

"Why?" Gillett asked. "I mean, I know why *I'm* committed to it, but why you? Just as a favor to me?"

"No," Clint said, "it's not just that. I sort of feel . . . obligated now."

"I don't understand."

"I can't say that I do, either," Clint said.

"Obligated to who?"

Clint thought a moment, and then said, "To the women whose lives we'll save by catching them."

Gillett thought about that himself for a moment and then nodded.

"You know," he said, "I think I can understand that pretty well."

"Yeah," Clint said, "so can I."

"I'll take the first watch," Gillett said. "I don't feel much like sleeping right now, anyway."

"Neither do I, to tell you the truth," Clint said.

They stared at each other, and then Clint said, "Well, what do you say? Do you think you want to do a little night riding?"

"Why not?" Gillett said. "It's better than just sitting here talking."

With that they set about breaking the camp they had set up not so long ago, then saddled their horses and started riding through the night.

As the sun was coming up, they came upon a cold camp. Clint dismounted and held his hand over the old campfire, checking for heat.

"No," he said, "it's cold."

"How long you figure?" Gillett asked, looking around.

"Three days," Clint said. "Could even be two."

"Two horses," Gillett said, pointing to the tracks in the dirt, which were pretty faint.

"Probably between two days and three," Clint said. "No more."

He looked up at Gillett, who said, "It's got to be them."

"These tracks are all we've got," Clint said, mounting up, "so let's go on that assumption and start following them."

"Sounds good to me," Gillett said. "Even if they're the wrong tracks, as long as we're going south we're headed in the right direction."

"You want to camp for breakfast?" Clint asked.

"No," Gillett said. "Not unless you do."

"How's your horse holding up?"

"Not as well as yours," Gillett admitted, "but we can rest him every so often without stopping to camp. Now that we've got some tracks to follow, let's just keep moving."

"Agreed," Clint said, "let's keep going."

TWENTY-FOUR

The Baca brothers camped for the night outside of a town called Big Fork, New Mexico.

"I don't see why we can't go into town," Enofre said. "There are women there, you know."

"That's why we're not going in," Abran said.

"I don't understand that."

"We can't take any chances, Enofre," Abran said. "Not after what happened in Never Bend."

"But—"

"Never mind," Abran said. "You stand the first watch and wake me in three hours."

"Three?"

"Yes," Abran said. "I want to start moving in six hours."

"Why?"

"Because by now that Ranger has been to Never Bend," Abran said. "He knows what happened, and he'll be on our trail."

"I want him to catch up to us," Enofre said.

"What?"

"I *want* him to catch up," the older brother said.

"Why?"

"I want to find out why he is after us so hard," Enofre said, "and then I want to kill him."

"You stand the first watch," Abran said again, "and wake me if you hear anything."

Abran rolled himself up in his blanket and lay there awake, thinking. He knew he was feeling what his brother was feeling. The urge was coming back, and it had never come back this soon. He seemed able to resist it more than his brother, though. He knew that if he let Enofre go into town—or if he even let him go near a woman—it would happen again.

What would he do, he wondered, when the urge became too much for Enofre to resist?

More to the point, what would he do when it became too much for *him*?

"I wonder what drives them to do what they do," Clint said.

They were camped for the night, they and the horses taking a much needed rest after having pushed for the better part of twenty-four hours.

"I've thought about that," Gillett said. "I've thought about it a lot, even more over the past couple of weeks. I can't figure it out. Is it possible that they *enjoy* what they do?"

"Why else would they do it?"

"I don't know," Gillett said with a shrug. "Maybe they *have* to do it."

"What do you mean, *have* to do it?"

"I don't know what I mean," Gillett admitted. "Maybe there's something inside them that *makes* them do . . . what they do."

"You mean . . . they can't help it?" Clint asked. "Like they don't have a choice?"

Again, Gillett could only shrug.

Clint thought about that for a while and then shook his head.

"I can't understand that," he said. "I've always taken responsibility for what I do with my life. I mean, I make my own decisions, nobody forces me to do what I do."

"What about something inside?"

"Are you trying to understand these men, Jim?" Clint asked.

Gillett passed a hand over his tired eyes and said, "I don't know what I'm trying to do, Clint. I really don't. I'm just . . . talking. It keeps me from screaming."

There was no question of riding through the night this time. They were both too tired, and so were the horses— although Clint thought that Duke could probably go a little further than the rest of them.

"I'll take the first watch," Clint said. "I think you need sleep a little more than I do."

Gillett looked at him and then said, "I'm not gonna argue with you, Clint."

"How's your head?"

For a moment Clint thought the Ranger would snap at him, but apparently Gillett was too tired to even do that.

"I've got a headache most of the time," he admitted.

"We probably should have had a doctor take a look at you."

"What for?" Gillett said.

"Maybe he'd say that you shouldn't be riding."

"And if he did say that?" Gillett asked, wrapping himself up in his blanket. "What do you think I'd do?"

"You'd probably just keep on riding."

"Right," Gillett said tiredly. "So what's the point of going to a doctor now?"

"No point, I guess," Clint said, "but if you drop dead on me, I'm going to leave you where you lay."

"That's fine with me," Gillett said, "as long as you keep going after the Bacas."

Clint was going to answer Gillett, but the Ranger had fallen asleep almost before the words had been out of his mouth.

He answered him anyway.

"You know," he said to the sleeping man, "I believe I would."

TWENTY-FIVE

It was in a town called Filmore, New Mexico, that the Bacas made their first mistake.

Actually, it was Enofre who made the critical error. They were both eating in a small café, talking about what they should do now and where they should go.

"The rest of the boys should be in Chapman now," Abran said. "We can send them a telegraph message from here to wait for us. Once we join up with them, we can ride into Ol' Mexico."

Abran made sure that no one was close enough to them to hear what they were talking about. That was why he always stopped talking when the waitress came by.

Enofre, however, was not as careful. The waitress was approaching the table when he asked, "Why do we have to join them in Chapman? Why don't we just meet them in Mexico?"

"Shhhh," Abran said as the waitress approached the table.

She was in her mid-thirties, a handsome woman who was no longer as slender as she had once been. Now she was full-bodied and mature, and she wore it well.

Abran appreciated how she looked, but to Enofre she was too fat. Enofre, after all, liked his women young and slender, like the whore he had killed in Never Bend.

"Can I get you gents anything else?" she asked.

"What is your name, *chica*?" Abran asked.

"Marian."

"Perhaps I could come back when you have finished work and answer that question then, eh?"

"I don't think so," she said. "Why don't you just answer it now."

"You do not want this one. She is much too fat," Enofre said to Abran.

"Oh sure," she said, "and you're every woman's dream, right?"

Enofre reached out and grabbed her arm, gripping it tightly.

"Hey . . ." she said, trying to pull away.

"Let her go," Abran said.

"Did you hear her?"

"Yes," Abran said, "and she is right, you are *not* every woman's dream. Let her go, Enofre!"

Enofre matched his brother's stare for a moment, then he released the woman's arm and looked away.

"You fellas gonna pay your check without any trouble?" she asked.

"We will pay you," Abran said slowly, "when we are finished."

"Fine," she said, and walked away. She hadn't liked the way they looked when they walked in, and seeing that they were twins had made it twice as bad. Now she was hoping that they would leave without any more trouble.

Walking back to the kitchen she thought, the sooner they leave for Chapman, the better she'd like it.

"You having some trouble out there?" the cook asked her.

The cook was over fifty, fat and balding, and he had his eye on her. She wondered what he'd do if she answered his question with a "yes."

Ah, he'd probably get himself killed trying to impress her.

"Nothing I can't handle, Frank," she said. "Don't worry about it."

As the waitress walked away, Abran said to his brother under his breath, "Damn it, you know we cannot afford to attract any attention. Not after what happened in Never Bend."

"You were the one who started talking to her," Enofre said defensively. "I don't know how you can like a woman like that. She is so fat and old."

"She is not fat and old," Abran said. "I just like my women a little older and with more meat than you do."

Enofre shook his head and said, "Fat."

"I prefer them," Abran said, taking money out of his pocket, "old enough to not need a father."

He dropped the money on the table and walked out, heading for the telegraph office.

Enofre stood up and hurried after his brother, trying to think of something to say in reply.

When the two Mexicans left, Marian went back to their table, hoping they had left enough money to cover the bill. Even if they hadn't, she was glad to see them go. As it turned out, they left just enough money and no tip. That suited her, as well.

By the time she got back to the kitchen, she forgot that she had heard them say they were going to a town called Chapman.

Days later, though, she would remember. She was like that. She heard the conversations that went on in the café and filed the information away without even realizing it, until something jogged her memory.

Like another conversation.

TWENTY-SIX

Two days later Clint Adams and James Gillett rode into Filmore, New Mexico. They were both wondering how far behind the Baca boys they were at that point.

"Pretty far, if we followed the wrong trail," Gillett said.

"Don't get so dejected," Clint said. "Like you said, we're probably going in the right direction even if we're following the wrong trail."

They had decided that the horses needed the night to rest, so they'd get a hotel room and get some rest themselves, as well. They also needed to buy some more coffee, and bacon and beans—even though they were both tired of bacon and beans.

They left the horses at the livery and went to the hotel to register. After that, they went to the saloon for some beer and got into a conversation with the bartender.

"Where can we get a good steak in this town?" Clint asked the man.

"Right down the street," the bartender said. "There's a little café with no name. Just go in and tell the waitress, Marian, that Joe sent you."

"What does that get us?" Clint asked.

The bartender grinned and said, "A smile with your food."

"Will it be worth it?"

"You tell me," the man said, "after you've seen Marian."

"Attractive, is she?" Gillett asked.

"If you like your women with some mileage on them," the bartender said, "and I do."

"I don't mind it myself," Clint said. "Let's go, Jim. I'm hungry."

"So am I," Gillett said. "Thanks for the beer, bartender."

"And the directions," Clint said.

"Come on back after you eat and let me know how it was," the man said.

"Why?" Clint asked, kidding. "Haven't you ever eaten there?"

"Me?" the man said. "No, never. I just send people there 'cause I like Marian. I eat here."

"Well . . . why don't *we* eat here?" Gillett said. "I mean, if they serve food."

"Mister," the bartender said, "I wouldn't recommend that *anyone* eat here!"

Clint nodded and said, "The café, it is."

When they entered the café, the first thing Clint noticed was the waitress.

Gillett didn't comment about her, but then he wasn't so long removed from the tragedy of his woman's death. Clint decided not to talk about women with him. He felt badly now about how Gillett must have felt when he was in the room next to Clint and Estralita.

The waitress came up to them and said, "Sit anywhere you can."

"Thanks," Clint said.

It was small, like most cafés Clint had been to in Western towns. They usually concentrated more on the food than on appearance.

They had to wait a few minutes, but then the woman came over to take their order.

"What can I get for you gents?"

"Are you Marian?" Clint asked.

"That's right," she said. "Don't tell me, let me guess. Joe sent you from the saloon?"

"How did you know that?"

She smiled and said, "He sends a lot of folks over. He's afraid that if they eat the food at the saloon they won't go there anymore, even to drink."

"Why does he worry about that?"

"He owns the place."

"And do you own this place?"

"Nope," she said. "I just work here."

"What do you suggest?" Clint asked.

"How about a couple of steaks?" she said. "The cook knows how to do them up just right, with onions and potatoes and—"

"I'm sold already," Clint said.

"Me, too."

"Two steaks," she said. "Comin' up."

"And a pot of coffee, please," Clint said.

"Before or after?"

"Both."

She laughed and said, "Comin' up."

As she walked away—and as Clint was watching her walk away—Gillett said, "Yes."

"Yes, what?"

"The bartender was right about her," he said. "She is very attractive."

Clint didn't quite know what to say to that. Since learning about the death of Gillett's woman, he wasn't quite sure how to act around him.

"Clint," Gillett said, "it's all right, you don't have to be so careful around me. If you like the way a woman looks, say so."

"I just thought—"

"I know what you thought," Gillett said. "Don't worry so much about it, all right?"

"Okay."

"By the way . . ."

"What?"

"She likes you."

"How do you know that?"

"You mean you can't tell when a woman likes you?" Gillett asked.

"Usually, yes," Clint said, "but we've only been here a few minutes."

"Wait," Gillett said, "you'll see."

"How?"

"Wait until the steaks come," the Ranger said. "Your plate will be more full than mine."

"Oh, come on."

"You'll see. . . ."

"She can't do that," Clint said.

"Why not?"

"She'd get fired."

Gillett shook his head and said, "I don't think so."

TWENTY-SEVEN

She brought them the coffee first, putting the pot
and two cups on the table between them. A few
minutes later, when she brought out their food, Clint
saw that Gillett was right. His plate had more potatoes
and onions on it, and even his steak seemed a little
larger.

"See?" Gillett said before she walked away. "I told
you."

"Told you what?" she asked. She looked back and
forth at them, as if she suspected that there was some
sort of joke going on.

"Oh, nothing . . ." Clint said, but Gillett wouldn't
let it go.

"I told my friend that his plate would have more
food on it than mine."

"Is there something wrong with your portion?" she
asked Gillett.

"Don't listen to him," Clint said.

The Ranger put both hands up and said, "No, no, I'm not complaining. I just told him that you liked him, and it would show up in his portion. That's all." He looked down at his plate and said, "This looks fine to me."

"Oh . . ." she said, and she looked directly into Clint's eyes.

"I know, I know," Clint said, "he's just being ridiculous."

"No, he's not," she said.

She laughed at the look that came over Clint's face.

"I'm sorry," she said, "but I'm real outspoken sometimes."

"That's nothing to apologize about," Clint said.

She put her hand on his shoulder, and he was impressed with the strength in her grip.

"Your friend is right," she said. "As soon as you walked in, do you know what I thought about?"

"What?"

"A bath."

"A bath?"

"Yes," she said, and then she touched his cheek and said, "With you," and walked away.

Clint looked across the table at Gillett, who seemed very interested in his meal. As Clint started to eat, though, Gillett said, "See?"

"Okay, okay," Clint said, and he was surprised to find that he was embarrassed.

TWENTY-EIGHT

The steaks were delicious, just red enough and tender enough. The potatoes and onions were perfect, and Marian even brought out a basket of biscuits.

"Those are from me," she said, smiling at Clint and touching his arm.

"Don't say anything," Clint said to Gillett, who was smiling.

"What was I gonna say?" the Ranger asked innocently. "Just that it must be hell being so . . . wanted. I mean, first Estralita—that sweet, young creature—and now Marian, this attractive, mature woman. You appeal to such a wide variety—"

"Just eat your food."

Actually, Clint appreciated the attentions of Marian more than those of Estralita. True, the Mexican girl had been young and eager, but he usually preferred older, more experienced women—the kind that Marian was certain to be.

After dinner she brought out another pot of coffee without being asked.

"Well," Gillett said, as she went back to the kitchen, "the service sure has been good, hasn't it?"

"She probably gives *everybody* good service," Clint said.

"Oh yeah?" Gillett asked. "Did you see anyone else get a basket of biscuits?"

"I don't see you complaining," Clint said.

"Oh, I'm not," Gillett said. "In fact, I think I want to eat in restaurants with you more often. I'll get better service that way."

"Why don't you take a walk?" Clint said. "And I'll pay the bill."

"Oh, I see," Gillett said, "you want me out of the way, right?"

"Right."

"Say no more," Gillett said. "I'm going to go back to the hotel and stay there."

"I'll be by later," Clint said. "I'll probably stop at the saloon for a while."

"Sure," Gillett said, standing up. "Listen, take all the time you need, okay? I won't be waiting up for you."

"Get out of here," Clint said.

Gillett left just as Marian came back from the kitchen and approached the table.

"Well," she said, "is there anything else I can get for you?"

"No," Clint said, "everything was very good—especially the service."

"Well," she said, "you know why that is, don't you?"

"Do I?"

"Oh," she said, giving him a long look, "I think you do. What's your name?"

"Clint."

"How long are you in town for?"

"Just overnight, I'm afraid."

"Well," she said, "then I have to be *real* forward, don't I? I mean, I don't have time to play hard to get, do I?"

"I guess neither of us do," he said.

"Then you're interested?"

"Oh, yes."

"Good," she said. "You know, I just *love* taking baths. I mean, I think the most erotic thing in the world is soapy water."

"Oh, really?"

"Well," she said, "*sharing* soapy water with someone is pretty erotic, isn't it?"

"Oh, yes."

She touched his arm then and said, "I have a bathtub in my room. It cost me, but then I don't spend money on anything else."

"I see."

"I finish up here at ten," she said. "Can you find something to do until then?"

"Three hours?" he said. "I think I can find a way to fill the time."

"Good," she said, "and then *I'll* find a way to fill your time after that."

He stood up, paid his bill, and said, "Marian, I think you already have."

Gillett went directly back to the hotel, removed his boots, and sat on the bed. He took his gun out and decided to clean it before he got some sleep. His head was aching, and he knew that Clint had been right when he said he should have seen a doctor. He didn't want to tell Clint, but in addition to the headaches, he was suffering from occasional bouts of double vision. Well, after he tracked down the Baca brothers there'd be plenty of time to go and see a doctor. Right now he only had time for one thing—hunting the men who had butchered his sister and his woman.

It was a true stroke of luck to have run into Clint Adams. Not only did he have someone to back his play, but it was the man known as the Gunsmith. He couldn't have asked for anything more than that, could he? Even if Clint's reputation wasn't *totally* deserved, he himself had seen enough to know that the man would more than hold his own when they finally caught up to the Bacas—whether they had their gang with them or not.

He finished cleaning his gun and replaced it in his holster. He worked on his rifle next, but right in the middle of it his vision started to blur.

"Damn!" he cursed. He dropped the rifle and placed the heels of his hands against his eyes and rubbed vigorously. He knew it wouldn't help. Nothing did. He usually just had to wait for it to pass—and luckily it had always passed pretty quickly, before Clint could ever notice that something was wrong.

He sat with his back against the bedpost and waited, and sure enough his vision cleared after about four or five minutes. He heaved a sigh of relief and tried not to think about what he would do if his vision ever blurred, and doubled . . . and then *didn't* clear.

He shook his head, dispelling any thoughts of that. He picked up his rifle and finished cleaning it, then reclined on the bed and tried to will himself to sleep. It was funny, but there were times when he just *couldn't* fall asleep, and times when he just *couldn't* wake up.

Jesus, he thought, rubbing one hand over his face, that was probably also a result of his head injury. Right now he just couldn't seem to even close his eyes, let alone fall asleep.

He got out of bed, walked to the window, moved the room's single chair in front of it, and sat down. Might as well watch what was going on down in the street, watch the town sort of go to sleep as it got later and later. Maybe once the town fell asleep, he could, too.

TWENTY-NINE

When Clint left the café he walked to the saloon, where the bartender remembered him.

"So?" the man asked.

"You were right, Joe," Clint said.

"About Marian?"

"Yes."

"What about the food?"

"The food was good, too."

"Well, good," the man said. "How about a beer on the house?"

"Sure," Clint said. "If you're offering, I'd be a fool not to take it."

"Besides," Joe said, putting the beer in front of him, "I know that you can't just drink one. If I give one away once in a while, I'm usually able to sell a few more right after it."

"Sounds like you've put a lot of thought into it," Clint said, lifting the beer.

"Gotta do something," Joe said. "I'm tryin' to make a decent living."

"You must do okay," Clint said, "owning the only saloon in town."

"Maybe," Joe said, "but I won't *always* own the only saloon in town. I mean, hopefully, the town will grow, and I want that. I also know that means that another saloon will probably open up. I'm just trying to build up enough good will to see me through."

"Well," Clint said, "you've got my vote. What are the chances of getting up a poker game, here?"

"If you wait about fifteen more minutes, a regular game will start up," Joe said, "and they usually make room for new blood."

Clint finished his beer and said, "Well, I might as well have another one while I'm waiting."

Joe smiled and said, "See what I mean?"

When the regular game started up, it turned out to be four town residents, who met every night to play for small stakes. Since Clint was just looking to kill time, he didn't care about the size of the stakes. When they warned him that it was a small game, he said it was okay, he didn't mind.

The stakes were two and four bits, and at that rate, over the course of the next two hours, he still managed to win fifty dollars.

"Well," he said, when it was nearing ten o'clock, "thanks for the game, gentlemen. I think it's time for me to turn in."

"Good," one of the players said, "maybe now somebody else can win a hand."

He wasn't complaining, though. In fact, they all
bade Clint good night and told him it had been a
pleasure playing with him.

Clint left the saloon and walked over to the café to
meet Marian.

When he reached the café, Marian was waiting for
him just inside the closed door. She opened it and
reached for him, grabbing him by the hand.

"Hey!" he said as she pulled him inside.

"Hurry, hurry," she said, pulling him along, "the
water's hot."

"Wha—"

She pulled him through the kitchen to the stairway
in the back.

"You live here?" he asked. "I thought you didn't
own the place."

"I don't live here," she said. "I live upstairs, though,
and I manage the café for the owner, who only comes
around about once a month to pay me and try to get
me into bed."

"And does he?"

"I'm very particular about who I keep company
with," she said. "Which reminds me . . . come on!"

She pulled him up the stairs and he found himself
in a room with a porcelain bathtub. The water in it
was steaming, and already soapy. The tub was easily
big enough to accommodate two people.

"Okay," she said, releasing him, "get out of those
clothes and let's get into the bath. I smell like steak
and onions."

"You smell fine to me," he said.

She moved closer to him, bumped his chest with her firm breasts, and pulled his head down so she could kiss him, thoroughly and wetly.

"See?" she said, giving his lips one last lick. "I even taste like frying meat."

"I'm not complaining," he said.

"Once we're in the bathtub you'll taste the difference," she promised, and she started to take off her clothes.

He didn't waste any time, then. He was anxious to have her keep her promise.

THIRTY

He watched with pleasure as she removed her dress, revealing her body to him. She was solidly built, with full breasts and hips. Her butt was smooth and rounded, looking almost like a perfect pear shape. Her nipples were a coppery color and erect.

He reached for her, his penis thickening, and she danced away, her breasts bobbing.

"Wait until we're in the tub."

"Well, then let's get in it!"

"Me, first."

He watched in fascination as she walked naked to the tub, lifted her leg to get in, and then the other leg. She lowered herself into the hot water.

"Oooh, that feels *soooo* gooood," she moaned, and he felt a rush at her tone of voice.

"Come on over here, Clint," she said, still in the same tone of voice. "Get in here with me and wash my back."

She didn't have to ask him twice.

He walked over and at first he was going to get into the tub opposite her, but then he decided it would be better to get in behind her.

"Move forward a little," he said, lifting his leg.

"What are you—oh, what a good idea," she said, and moved forward to let him in.

He got into the tub and sat down behind her, with his legs stretched out alongside of her. The tub was just wide enough for this. His rigid penis was pressed against her back, and she leaned back against him, moaning.

"Ooh, that feels good."

He took the soap from her and began to soap her back, her shoulders, and her neck. She closed her eyes and relaxed as his hands kneaded her, and then he surprised her by sliding his hands around to her front and cupping her breasts.

"Ohh!" she said, and then, "Oooh!" as he caressed her nipples with his thumbs.

He began to wash her breasts, rubbing the palms of his soapy hands over them.

"Oh, Jesus," she said, with her head against his shoulder. "Christ, I've got to . . . reach you . . . oh, shit, I can't—" she said, as she tried to reach behind her for him.

"I can reach you, though," he said, and ran his hands over her thighs.

"Ooh, not fair, not . . . fair," she said, as he started to rub the inside of her thighs.

He soaped his hands good again, in front of her, and then slid one hand down over her breasts and her belly and began to rub the hair between her legs.

"Oh, God . . ." she said, "you wouldn't . . . would you?"

Yes, he would, he thought, and plunged his hand down further.

When his fingers touched her privates she gave a little leap that caused some splashing, and then he was rubbing his fingers over her. She stretched her legs out and let out a loud moan, and then suddenly he felt her shudder as a wave of pleasure shot through her.

"Shit," she said, "that's about all I can take of that. . . ."

She moved then, bending her knees and sliding away from him, then standing, turning, and straddling him. She reached for him in the water, found him, and held him firmly in one hand, then lowered herself down on him, taking him inside.

"Oooh," she moaned as he entered her, and then she sat down on him and he was buried in her to the hilt.

In this position he was able to kiss her, which he did. Their tongues intertwined, and she moaned as she rode him up and down. At one point she pulled her mouth away from his and dropped her head back so that he could slide his lips and tongue over her neck. He did that, then moved to her shoulders, and finally to her slippery breasts. He caught one nipple in his mouth and sucked it, then switched to the other one. Meanwhile, she continued to bounce up and down in his lap, moaning and crying out, until she was bouncing so violently that he could no longer keep contact with her breasts. Also, she was splashing so much that the water was going on the floor. She didn't seem to mind that, and he wondered how she'd feel if the tub tipped over with them in it, spilling gallons of water all over the place. . . .

Suddenly, she stopped bouncing, and he felt her insides clamp down around him. It was more than he could stand and suddenly he was exploding inside of her just as another wave of pleasure coursed through her. . . .

"Drying," she said, a little later, "is almost as good as washing."

They had remained in the water, kissing and touching, until the water turned tepid, and then she got out first and went to fetch some towels. Now they were both out of the tub, and he took a towel from her.

"Let me dry you," he said.

"All right," she said, "and then I'll dry you."

He started behind her, drying her back and her butt, lingering over the firm globes of her ass, and then turned her around and dried her neck and shoulders, and then her breasts. He squeezed her through the towel and could feel her nipples. She kissed him then, and it developed into a long kiss.

"Wait . . ." he said, pulling his mouth away finally. "Let me finish drying you."

He got on his knees and dried first one leg and then the other. Finally, he began to rub the towel over her privates, and she leaned into the pressure of his hand.

"Mmmm," he said, "you're so clean and fresh now."

He leaned forward and kissed her belly, running his tongue over her navel, and then he lowered his mouth just a little and began to lick her.

"Oh, Christ," she groaned, "oh, Jesus. . . ."

As he continued to lick her, and kiss her, her legs suddenly went weak and she had to lean on his shoulders or fall down.

He entered her then with his tongue, in quick little thrusts, then found her clit and began to lash it back and forth.

"Ohhhh, shit," she said, "God, you've got to fuck me . . . now, Clint . . . come on . . ." she said, and she started beating him on the shoulders to get his mouth off of her.

"I'm not dry yet," he said, but she pushed him back so that he was lying on the floor on his back.

She straddled him and took him inside of her again and said, "So what?" She picked up a towel then and said, "I'll dry you this way."

THIRTY-ONE

Later—when they finally made it to her bed—
they lay side by side, with her head nestled on his
shoulder.

"It's too bad you're leaving town tomorrow," she
said sadly.

"Yes," he said, although he didn't really think so. If
he stayed, she'd either wear him out, or drown him.

"Can't you stay a little longer?"

"I wish I could," he lied, "but I can't."

"Because of your friend?"

"Yes."

"I saw the badge on his chest," she said. "He's a
Texas Ranger, isn't he?"

"That's right."

"Hunting someone?"

"Yes."

"And you're helping him?"

"Yes."

She hesitated a moment, then lifted her head and said, "Boy, you don't talk much, do you?"

He looked at her, touched her cheek, and said, "I wasn't aware that you enticed me up here to talk."

"Enticed, huh?"

"That's right."

She studied him in the dark for a moment and then nodded and said, "Yeah, I guess I did do that, didn't I?"

"You certainly did," he said, "with promises of hot, soapy water and . . ."

"And what?"

"Just . . . *and*."

"Well," she said, running her hand down his chest, "how did you like the *and*?"

"It was fine."

She had her hand on his belly when he said that and moved it to his side to pinch about an inch of flesh.

"Just fine, huh?"

"All right, all right," he said, "it was great, wonderful, magnificent."

She released his flesh and said, "I'll accept magnificent."

She put her head on his shoulder again.

"Who is he hunting?" she asked.

"Two men," Clint said.

"What did they do?"

There was really no harm in telling her.

"They killed his sister and the woman he was going to marry—along with a lot of other women."

"God," she said, "no wonder he's hunting them—

and no wonder you're helping him. You're gonna miss Christmas, though."

"I know," he said.

"Won't your family be sorry?" she asked. "Your wife, and all?"

"I don't have a wife," he said.

"Any family, at all?"

"No."

"Me neither," she said. "Christmas is one of my least favorite times of the year."

"I don't necessarily feel that way."

"You must have friends to spend it with, then."

"Some."

"Actually" she said, "that's what you're doing now, isn't it? Spending it with a friend?"

"Yeah," he said, "I guess you could say that."

They lay quietly for a while, and just when he thought she might have fallen asleep, she spoke again.

"Does he know who did it?" she asked. "I mean, does he know who the men are?"

"Yes," Clint said. "A couple of brothers named Baca. Do you know them?"

"Baca?" she repeated. "No, I never heard the name. Mexicans, huh?"

"That's right."

"And brothers," she said. "You know, there were a couple of Mexicans here a few days ago."

That got his attention.

"Where?"

"Here," she said. "They ate in the café. I thought there was gonna be trouble because one of them liked me. The other one didn't, and they argued over it."

"Did you hear their names?"

"I didn't hear Baca, if that's what you mean."

"What about Enofre or Abran?"

"Abran?" she said. "No . . . but what was that other one?"

"Enofre."

"That sounds *almost* like what I heard. I mean, I wasn't sure what they were saying."

"Were they brothers?" he asked.

"They must have been."

"Why do you say that?"

"Because they looked alike."

"Close enough to be brothers?"

"Clint," she said, "they were close enough to be the same person."

"What do you mean?"

"I mean," she said, lifting her head and looking at him, "they were identical. They were twins."

THIRTY-TWO

"The men you're looking for," she said, "are they twins?"

"I don't know," he said. "Gillett—my friend—never said."

"Maybe he doesn't know."

"Maybe," he said, "and maybe not."

Clint thought about that for a few moments. Could Gillett have known they were twins and never mentioned it to him?

"I don't suppose you heard these men say where they were going, did you?"

"As a matter of fact," she said, "one of them said something about sending a telegram to Chapman."

"Chapman?" he said. "Where's that?"

"About three days ride south of here," she said. "That puts it about a day from the border."

"Jesus!" he said.

He literally bounded out of bed.

126

"Wha—" she said.

"Get dressed," he told her.

"It's the middle of the night," she said. "What's wrong?"

He went to the window and looked outside. The sky in the east was just beginning to show signs of becoming light. Morning was coming.

"It's not the middle of the night," he said, pulling his pants on.

"Clint—"

"Marian," he said, "you just told me something very important. I have to go and talk to Gillett. Can you meet us in an hour?"

"In an hour?" she said. "It won't even be light by then."

"I'll buy you breakfast."

"Where?" she demanded. "This place makes the best breakfast in town."

"Pick a place, then," he said, putting his shirt on. "It's important that Gillett hears what you've just told me."

"Oh, all right," she said, "but bring him here. I'll make breakfast."

"Can you cook?"

"Of course I can cook," she said, "but you're going to have to promise me something if I do this."

"What?" he asked, strapping on his gun.

"When this is all over, and you've caught those men, you have to come back here . . ."

"And?"

"And take another bath with me."

He leaned over the bed and said, "I think I can promise that."

She reached up, put her hands behind his head, and pulled his mouth down to hers. They kissed hungrily, and the kiss went on so long that he entertained thoughts of getting back into bed with her.

But he didn't. . . .

"I have to go," he said, slipping from her grasp. "We'll be downstairs in an hour."

"Oh, all right!"

"Thanks," he said, and went down the steps two at a time.

Outside Clint was turning over the information in his mind. If the men Marian had seen *were* the Bacas, and they were on their way to this town Chapman, Clint and Gillett could leave early this morning and ride hell-for-leather to get there and maybe catch up to them before they *left* Chapman.

This would probably be the closest Gillett would have gotten to them in a long time.

As he crossed the street to the hotel, he wondered if the Bacas were going there to meet the rest of their gang.

THIRTY-THREE

Clint pounded on Gillett's door until the man opened it. He was standing there naked and groggy, a sight to behold.

"Jesus," Clint said, "put some pants on."

"What the hell time is it?"

"Time to get some good news, for a change," Clint said. He entered the room and shut the door while Gillett struggled into his pants.

He stopped short with one leg in and one leg out, staring at the window.

"It's still dark!"

"Not as far as we're concerned," Clint said.

Gillett finished putting his pants on and sat down on the bed.

"What are you so excited about?"

Clint told him.

"And she knows they were the Baca boys?"

"No," he said, "all she knows is that they were brothers."

"How does she know that?"

"Because they were twins."

"Twins?"

"That's right," Clint said. "Are the Baca boys twins, that you know of, Jim?"

"I never heard—but wait. That's why the descriptions were always the same. I just assumed it was because they were brothers—but twins! I never suspected."

"Well, we still might be wrong," Clint said, "but I think this is worth a try. What do you think?"

"I think we better find out what kind of telegram they sent."

"Good idea," Clint said. "We'll have to get the key operator out of bed, though."

"Before we can do that," Gillett said, "we have to find out who he is."

"And before we can do that," Clint said, "you have to finish getting dressed. Come on, Marian's making breakfast, and I'm sure she can tell us who the operator is and where to find him."

When they got to the café the front door was open and they could smell food frying.

"Marian!" Clint called as they entered.

"I'll be right out," she said. "Sit at the big table."

There was only one big table and that was the one in the middle of the room. It was the only table that could accommodate more than two people. They sat down, and she came out with a big tray of food. Eggs, potatoes, bacon, and biscuits.

"Frank's gonna go crazy when he finds out I used his kitchen," she said.

"Clint told me what you saw and heard, Miss—"

"Just Marian."

"Marian," Gillett said. "Can you think of anything else?"

"No," she said. "I've thought about it, but that's all I can remember."

"It's enough to get us started," Clint said. "We need one more thing, Marian."

"What's that?"

"The telegraph key operator."

"That'd be Clarence," she said, "Clarence Holden. He lives at the hotel you're staying in."

Clint and Gillett exchanged chagrined glances.

"We could have gotten that from the desk clerk," Clint said.

"Let's go and talk to him."

"Oh no you don't," Marian said. "If I'm gettin' in trouble for cooking this food, you're sure as shootin' gonna eat it."

"But—"

"It'll take ten minutes," she said.

They looked at each other, then shrugged and started to eat.

THIRTY-FOUR

For the second time that morning Clint was pounding on a hotel door. The desk clerk had been reluctant to give them Clarence Holden's room number, but a few dollars had solved that problem.

"What is it?" a voice called out.

"We want to talk to you."

"Who is it?"

"Come on, come on, open up," Gillett said. "Texas Rangers."

"Texas . . . what?"

A small man opened the door and peered out at them from behind wire frame glasses. He was wearing a pair of red long johns.

"Texas Rangers, did you say?" he asked, looking them both up and down.

"That's right."

"This is New Mexico."

"So I took a wrong turn," Gillett said. "Are you the telegraph key operator? Clarence?"

"That's right," the man said, "but I didn't do nothin'."

"We know you didn't," Gillett said. "I want to ask you some questions about two men who sent a telegraph message a couple of days ago."

"How am I supposed to remember—"

"You'll remember these men," Gillett said. "They were Mexicans, and they were twins."

"They were *what*?"

"They looked exactly alike," Clint said.

"Oh, them!" Clarence said. "Yeah, sure, I remember them."

"Where did they send their telegraph message to?" Clint asked.

"Gee, I don't know if I remember . . ." the man said, scratching his head.

"Was it Chapman?" Gillett asked. "A town called Chapman?"

"Yeah, that was it," the man said, pointing, "it *was* Chapman."

"All right," Clint said, "now this part is very important, Clarence. What did the message say? Can you remember?"

"Do you think I remember—" Clarence started to complain, but Gillett cut him off.

"Think, man!" Gillett said, grabbing the man by the front of his underwear.

"Hey, mister, take it easy," Clarence said, trying to pull away, but he stopped when Clint waved a five-dollar bill under his nose.

"Try and remember," Clint said.

"Well," he said, thinking hard, "it was something about waiting for them and not leaving for Mexico until they got there, him and his brother. I remember now. They was arguing over how to word it."

"You remember who they sent it to?" Clint asked.

The man thought, eyeing the money, but then shrugged and said, "Naw, I don't remember that."

"That's okay," Gillett said, "you remembered enough. Thanks."

Clint gave him the five dollars and said, "Go on back to sleep."

"Thanks," Clarence said, and shut the door.

"We've got to go," Gillett said as they went back downstairs. "If Chapman's two days away, then they're already there. If we ride hard, we can make it in a day and a half. Maybe they'll spend a day in Chapman and that'd put us a half a day behind them."

"Let's hope the livery stable is open this early," Clint said, "or we'll have to find out where the liveryman lives and get *him* out of bed."

The livery stable was already open, so they saddled their horses and then rode over to the hotel to pick up the rest of their belongings. As they rode past the café, Marian was standing outside.

"Remember our deal, Clint Adams!" she called out. "And good luck!"

"What deal was that?" Gillett asked.

"Oh, I made her a promise to get her to cooperate," Clint said.

"What kind of promise?"

"That I'd come back and take a bath with her."

Gillett stared at him, then shook his head and said, "Women are strange people."

THIRTY-FIVE

In the town of Chapman, New Mexico, one day's ride from the Mexican border, the Baca brothers were just awakening. They had arrived the day before and had met up with the five members of their gang.

Their gang—their childhood friend, Carlos Montanez, and the others—had been preparing to leave for Mexico when they received the telegraph message from Enofre and Abran, telling them to stay there and wait for them.

When the brothers arrived they found the five men at the cantina, and there was much hugging and backslapping, especially between the Bacas and Montanez.

"It is good to see you both," Montanez said. "We thought we were going to meet you in Ol' Mexico in a few weeks."

"Plans have changed," Abran said.

"Why?"

136

"I will tell you later," Abran said, "after we have eaten and drunk."

So they all ate and drank—and they drank too much, so they never had a chance to talk the night before.

Now this morning Enofre asked, "What are you going to tell them?"

"I will tell Carlos the truth," Abran said. "The others need not be told anything."

"Not even that a Texas Ranger is on our trail?" Enofre asked.

"That we will tell them," Abran said. "In fact, we might even leave the four of them here, just in case the Ranger gets this far. You and me and Carlos, we will go ahead and ride into Ol' Mexico."

"Surely the Ranger will not be able to get past Marco and Ramon and the others."

"Yes," Abran said, "surely. Come on, we have to meet Carlos for breakfast."

"Aiiee," Enofre said, holding his head, "we drank a lot last night. I did not even have a woman."

"No women in this town, Enofre!" Abran snapped.

His tone was so sharp that his brother looked up at him.

"I mean it," Abran said. "You can have all the women you want when we are in Mexico. There will be no more women here."

"And in Mexico," Enofre asked, "will we be able to have our way with the women? I mean *our* way?"

"We will have to stop that, Enofre," Abran said. "That has to end."

"*Sí*," Enofre said, "you say that now, but what happens when we *need* them—"

"That will have to change, Enofre!" Abran said again.

"*Sí*, my brother," Enofre said. "When it changes for you, it will change for me, eh?"

Abran knew, as they left their hotel room, that this was not true. He was not like Enofre. *He* could stop. He always knew that he could stop whenever he wanted to. It was Enofre he was worried about.

After all, Enofre—when it came to women—was an animal.

As it turned out, Abran and Carlos had breakfast together. Enofre said he did not feel like eating and wanted to go for a walk. Abran met Carlos in the hotel dining room.

"What happened?" Carlos asked.

Abran shook his head.

"He is out of control."

"And you, Abran?"

Abran looked at Carlos and said, "I can control it, Carlos. He cannot."

"How many?"

"It does not matter how many women we—he—killed," Abran said. "What matters is that there is a Texas Ranger tracking us."

"All the way here?" Carlos asked in surprise. "Outside of Texas?"

"Yes."

"Why?"

"We do not know," Abran said.

"What do you want to do?"

He told Carlos what he had decided, that Marco, Ramon, and the others would remain behind and wait for the Ranger.

"If he is not here in four days, then he is probably not coming," he finished. "Then they will be able to join us."

"All right," Carlos said, "But what is going to happen in Mexico?"

"We will have to watch Enofre," Abran said. "We will have to watch him very carefully."

"You mean like now?" Carlos asked. "When he has gone for a walk by himself?"

"Wait," Abran said.

He sat quietly for a moment, and then he felt it. Yes, it was there, the urge, down deep inside of him. Enofre would be feeling it even more.

"We must find him!" he said, and they got up and left the hotel.

THIRTY-SIX

Clint and Gillett rode their horses hard and made good time—even though Clint had to be careful that Duke didn't run the legs right off of Gillett's gray.

They rode even after dark, slowing the pace so that the animals wouldn't step in any chuckholes and break their legs. Of course, it impeded their progress, but losing one of the horses would have impeded it even more.

When they reached a point from where they could see the town, they stopped and dismounted, but not to rest the horses. The animals could rest when they got to town. No, they wanted a little bit of a rest themselves. When they rode into town, they wanted to be in some semblance of shape to handle whatever they came up against.

"A day," Gillett said. "Twenty-four hours in the saddle. I can't remember the last time I rode for that long."

"Well," Clint said, "it'll be worth it if they're still here, or if we're just behind them."

Gillett was looking over his gray.

"He's not going to be worth much after this," he said. "If we have to keep trailing them I'm going to need a new horse."

"I'm sorry."

"Like you said," Gillett said, "it'll be worth it if we catch up to them. Your horse looks okay, though."

Clint patted the big gelding's neck.

"He's got a lot of stamina," he said proudly.

Gillett looked at the sky and said, "It'll be light soon. We should probably ride in just before that. We might get in undetected."

"They won't be so hard to find," Clint said, "not if they're identical."

"I wish I had known that before," Gillett said. "It's the kind of information that could have made all the difference."

"Well," Clint said, "we know it now. That's all that matters."

They sat down together on the ground, every bone in their bodies aching, every muscle sore.

"We'll sit here for about half an hour," Clint said, "and then we'll move in. I think that's about all we can afford."

"I hope they're down there, Clint," Gillett said, with feeling. "By God, I hope they're still there."

In the town Marco Ramirez and Ramon Valdez were watching the street. Across the street, watching from that side, were the other two members of the gang, Eduardo Lopez and the only gringo in the group, Dave Ledbetter.

"How will we know this man when we see him?" Valdez wondered aloud.

"He is a Texas Ranger," Ramirez said. "He will be wearing that Ranger badge on his chest."

"Ah," Valdez said, "it will make for a good target to shoot at, no?"

"*Sí*," Ramirez agreed, "that it will, Ramon."

"I hope he comes today," Valdez said. "I do not want to spend another three days in this town. There is nothing to do here."

"Enofre," Ramirez said, "he found something to do here, didn't he?"

"The woman?" Valdez said. He made a face. "I cannot see wasting a woman like that. I mean, rape yes. Most of them want it that way, but to kill her . . ."

"Never mind," Ramirez said. "We follow Abran and we make a lot of money. If his brother is a little strange, who are we to judge?"

"We are lucky that the sheriff did not connect us with them, though," Valdez said, "or we would not be sitting here right now, waiting."

"The sheriff of this town is a *puta*," Ramirez said, spitting. "For enough money he looks the other way. I am not worried about him."

"But the town," Valdez said, "the people, they are upset—"

"Before they can connect us with Enofre, we will be gone," Ramirez said. "Stop worrying, Ramon." He tipped his hat down over his eyes and said, "Keep watching the street. Let me know if anyone comes."

They sat that way for a few moments, and then Valdez started to get fidgety, not liking the silence.

"Marco?"

"Hmm?"

"Do you think he will come today?"

"Enofre and Abran said that this man has been hunting them like . . . like a mad dog. If he has the scent like that, he will be along soon. Do not worry."

"I have never killed a Texas Ranger before," Valdez said.

"I have killed lawmen before," Ramirez said with a worldly shrug of his shoulders. "They die the same as any other man."

"All right," Gillett said, "it's time to ride on in. Let's get it over with."

They stood up, turned their horses around, and mounted up.

"What do you think?" Gillett asked. "Ride in this way, or circle around and come in from the other side?"

"The other side," Clint said. "If they met up with the rest of their gang here, they might be watching the street for us."

They urged their horses on—Gillett's mount taking more urging than Duke—and started to circle around the town. Chapman wasn't very big, and it still wouldn't be totally light by the time they reached the other side.

"The more I think about it," Clint said, "the more I like this idea. If the Bacas met up with their men here, they'd feel pretty confident to just wait and see when you arrived."

"But they don't know about you," Gillett said. "Maybe we should ride in separately."

"I don't think that's necessary," Clint said. "I think we're doing the right thing by coming in from the south rather than the north. Besides, even if they see us, there being two of us might make them think twice before acting. It might just give us an edge."

"An edge," Gillett said. "If there are a lot of them, that's something we're definitely going to need on our side."

THIRTY-SEVEN

When they reached the south end of town, Gillett leaned forward and patted his exhausted mount on the neck.

"He's about to collapse," he said. "Poor old guy. Sorry we had to push you so hard."

"So let's stop pushing him," Clint said.

"What do you mean?" Gillett asked. "We're already here."

"Why don't we walk in?" Clint suggested. "There's an even better chance of going undetected that way."

"Sounds good to me," Gillett said, after a moment. "If they're laying for us, we just might get the jump on them this way."

They dismounted, walked their horses right to the edge of town, and left them there. Gillett didn't even bother to tie his off. The animal was too tired to go any further on his own anyway.

"Let's split up, after all," Clint said. "You go across

145

the street, and we'll start walking together. Let's keep an eye on each other, so if one of us sees something he can tip the other one off to it."

"Right," Gillett said. "Good luck."

"You, too."

Gillett made his way across the street and looked back at Clint. They waved to each other and then started walking, making as little noise as possible.

All of the doorways and windows that Clint passed were dark. The town was still a couple of hours from waking up. With the streets as empty as they were right now, it would be easy to see if someone was waiting to ambush them.

Clint kept looking across at Gillett, just in case the Ranger saw something before he did.

That wasn't the case, though. It was Clint who noticed something first. In fact, he *smelled* something. He sniffed the air and realized it was cigarette smoke.

He waited for Gillett to look across at him and then made a "slow down" motion with his hands, and pointed up ahead of them. Gillett nodded, and they both slowed their progress.

Clint moved forward cautiously and finally saw the two men. They were sitting on the boardwalk, out of sight behind some crates. One of them was smoking while the other was watching the street to the north. Clint noticed that while one of them was Mexican, the other was American.

He looked across at Gillett, who was already looking at him and holding up two fingers. Apparently there were two men on his side of the street, as well.

Okay, that made things even. He was going to have

to take care of the men on this side, while Gillett handled the men on the other side.

He waved at Gillett, and they both started to move in.

Gillett's vision had not blurred recently, and he had been starting to think that the situation would not reoccur. However, it chose *this* particular moment to come back.

He was closing in on the two men ahead of him, who were still looking the other way, when suddenly his vision blurred. It was *so* sudden that it made him dizzy and threw his balance off. He staggered and knocked over a couple of barrels. The ensuing racket alerted not only the two men he was stalking, but the two across the street, as well.

They turned and when they saw him they drew their guns.

From across the street Clint saw Gillett stagger. Instinctively, he knew that something had happened to him, that the man hadn't simply been clumsy.

Clint saw the two men across the street draw their guns and knew that they were going to fire at Gillett while he was helpless. Ignoring the two men on his side of the street, Clint raised his gun and fired across.

He fired very quickly, pulling trigger four times, and all of his shots went true.

Gillett heard the shots and had the presence of mind to throw himself prone on the ground. There was nothing else he could do. If he fired, he would be

doing so blindly, with just as much chance of hitting
Clint as anyone else.

While he was lying on the ground, his vision cleared
almost as suddenly as it had blurred.

Clint knew that by firing across the street he had
given away his position to the men on his side of the
street. He turned to face them with two bullets left in
his gun, and saw that they were already facing him,
and already firing.

He steeled himself for the impact of the bullets even
as he pulled the trigger of his own gun.

Gillett got to his knees and looked across the street.
Daylight had come, seemingly just in those moments
that he'd been blinded, and he saw the two men turn
and fire at Clint. Knowing he was too late, he raised
his gun and fired at them, anyway.

Clint felt one bullet strike him in the left arm, and
then one of his shots hit home. The man spun away,
but the shot was not fatal. Suddenly, there was firing
from across the street, and he knew that Gillett was
back in the fray. The Ranger's shots struck the second
man once, twice, and then a third time, and the man
was propelled back into the glass window behind him.
The glass shattered and showered down on him, but
he was far from caring. The glass was cutting up a
corpse.

It was suddenly quiet, and Clint realized that he'd
been hit just the once, in his left arm. Gillett was back
on his feet across the street, apparently uninjured. The

other four men were down, and at least one of them was alive because he was making moaning sounds.

Well, one hit, he thought, that's not bad.

On the other hand, one was enough.

It hurt like a bastard!

THIRTY-EIGHT

The sounds of the shoot-out had managed to wake the town up, including the sheriff. One of the gang had survived, and both he and Clint were taken over to the doctor's office. Gillett, meanwhile, went to the sheriff's office to explain everything to the local lawman.

"This is great," the sheriff said. His name was Logan. He was in his late thirties and had been sheriff of Chapman for about two years. There'd been more excitement in the past couple of days than in all that time.

"First we have a woman murdered, and now this," Logan said.

"Wait a minute," Gillett said, "what's this about a woman being murdered?"

"Yeah, one of the local whores," Logan said. "She wasn't even working. Somebody grabbed her off the street, pulled her into an alley, raped her, and then— Jesus, he bit her all over and strangled her."

"Any witnesses to who did it?" Gillett asked.

"Not a one," Logan said. "I'm hoping it was just some crazy cowpoke passing through."

"What about those four we just shot it out with?" Gillett asked. "What do you know about them?"

"Not much," Logan admitted. "They been in town for almost two weeks. I thought they were waiting for someone. As a matter of fact, there *was* five of them. The other one must have left."

"Any other strangers in town?" Gillett asked.

"A couple, but they only stayed a few days. Rode out yesterday, as a matter of fact."

Gillett nodded. That would have been the Bacas, and they probably rode out with the fifth gang member.

"These four the ones you were after?" Logan asked.

"I guess we were the ones *they* were after," Gillett said. "They were laying for us."

"Well," Logan said, "I don't know the whole story, and I probably never will."

"All you have to do is keep the one that's left in your cell," Gillett said.

"For what?"

"He tried to kill us!"

"Seems to me you fellas were trying to kill each other," Logan said. "Fact is, you killed three of them. All I want is for the three of you to get out of town."

"Did you look into the possibility that one of those men might have killed the girl?"

"I did," Logan said. "I questioned them. They said they were all together the whole time."

"And you believed them?"

Logan spread his hands and said, "I can't prove otherwise."

"Is the town pretty upset about the girl?" Gillett asked.

"Some of them are," Logan said. "Others say she was a whore and askin' for it."

"Jesus," Gillett said, shaking his head, "nice town."

"It was," Logan said, "until you and your friends started shootin' it up. Do me a favor, Ranger. Take your dispute someplace else."

"Don't worry," Gillett said, "we'll be leaving just as soon as my friend gets patched up, and I can buy a new horse."

"Today?"

"Definitely today," Gillett said. "I've got no reason to stay in this town, Sheriff."

"Glad to hear it," Logan said.

Gillett walked to the door and said, "Not as glad as I am to say it."

The doctor worked on the surviving gang member, an American named Ledbetter.

"How is he?" Clint asked.

"He'll make it," the doctor said, "but he's not gonna be traveling for a while."

The man turned away from the table where Ledbetter was lying semiconscious and said, "Okay, let's take a look at that arm."

He tore the sleeve of Clint's shirt away from the wound and examined it.

"It's not bad," he said. "It didn't go all the way through, or you might have had a messy exit wound. I'll just dig it out and patch you up. You should be good as new. You're not plannin' on ridin' in the next day or two, are you?"

"As a matter of fact," Clint said, "I'm riding out today."

"You just rode in," the doctor said while he worked. "You're givin' new meanin' to the phrase, 'just passin' through.' "

"That's exactly what I'm doing," Clint said.

"Hang on tight while I get this bullet," the doctor said. "You want somethin' for the pain?"

"Just get it out, Doc."

"You been shot before, I suppose."

"A time or two."

The doctor set to work with his probe, found the bullet, and then extracted it. In record time he staunched the bleeding and wrapped the wound.

"Thanks, Doc," Clint said. "What do I owe you?"

"We can take care of that on your way out," the doctor said. "I'll be in my office. Sit here awhile before you leave. You might experience some dizziness. When you feel up to it, then come and see me."

"All right."

The doctor left, and Clint looked over at the supine man on the table. He got up and walked over to the man.

"Hey," he said softly, and then a little louder, "Hey!"

He was careful not to speak loud enough for the doctor to hear him.

Finally, the man's eyes fluttered open.

"Close call, huh, friend?" Clint said. "We were lucky we got you before you got us."

"Go . . . away . . ." the man said.

"Sorry, I can't do that," Clint said. "I'm looking for the Bacas, friend. You know, those sick buddies of yours who like to kill women?"

The man looked at him and said, "You don't know anything about it."

"I know I don't," Clint said. "Why don't you tell me about it?"

The man closed his eyes and for a moment Clint thought he had fallen asleep or passed out, but then he opened them again.

"Go . . . away . . ." he said.

"Not yet," Clint said. "I'll be back."

THIRTY-NINE

Clint was settling up with the doctor when Gillett appeared.

"Excuse me," the doctor said and went to check on his other patient.

"How are you doin'?" Gillett asked.

"I'm okay," Clint said. "What did you get from the sheriff?"

"Not much," Gillett said, and then gave Clint a rundown of his conversation with the man.

"So they did it again while they were here, huh?" Clint said when Gillett finished.

"Looks like it."

"I wonder what the general mood of the town is," Clint said.

"I mentioned that to the sheriff," Gillett said. "I got the impression it's about half and half."

"Yeah, well maybe we can use one half to our advantage."

155

"What do you mean?"

The doctor came out then and Clint said, "We need to talk to your patient, Doc."

When the man on the table opened his eyes this time he was looking up at two men, not one.

"How're you doing, friend?" Clint asked.

"Go . . . 'way. . . ."

"Can't do it," Clint said. "We got some bad news for you. See, you're going to live."

The man laughed shortly, which caused him some pain, and he winced.

"That's . . . bad . . . news?" he asked.

"It is for you," Clint said. "See, the town is up in arms about this woman who got killed. Seems they want to hang somebody for it. So guess what?" Clint laughed and said, "We're going to give them you."

"W-what?"

"Yeah," Clint said. "We figure if we can't get the Bacas, we might as well tell the townspeople that you were with them. They probably won't care that you didn't actually kill her yourself. They're just looking for somebody to string up."

"You can't."

"Sure we can," Gillett said. "As a matter of fact, they might not even hang you. They might just tear you apart with their bare hands."

"There's a mean mob outside right now," Clint said. "We've got to go out and talk to them."

The injured man closed his eyes, then opened them and asked, "W-what do you . . . want from me?"

"The Bacas," Gillett said. "Where were they going from here?"

"If I tell you, they'll . . . kill me."

"And if you don't tell us," Clint said, "this town will kill you. You know, if they come in here to get you, there isn't going to be much you can do to stop them. Not while you're lying here on this table."

"Jesus . . ." the man said, closing his eyes.

"All you have to do is tell us where they are," Gillett said. "Then we ride out after them, and you go free."

"No . . . jail?" the man asked.

"Free as a bird, friend," Gillett said. "If we can put our hands on the Baca brothers, nobody'll be interested in you."

"What do you say?" Clint asked.

The man's eyes closed again as he thought, and when he opened them, he nodded.

"San Genero?" Gillett said when they left the injured man alone. "I never heard of it."

"I think I have," Clint said. "I think it's a small town about three or four miles from the border."

"Well, that makes sense," Gillett said. "They'll probably think they're safe once they cross the border, and they wouldn't want to go too far into the country."

"You don't think they'll kill in their own country?" Clint asked.

"It hasn't been their pattern."

"I don't know," Clint said. "It seems to me their pattern is gone, Jim."

"What do you mean?"

"They seem to be out of control."

"I guess," he said. "What do you think that fella in there meant when he said they couldn't help themselves? That they didn't *want* to kill, but they *had* to?"

"I don't know," Clint said. "I guess that would be for some doctor who could look inside their heads to figure out."

"Well," Gillett said, "there ain't no doctor who's going to have that chance. I can guarantee that. We'd better get going. I've got to buy a new horse."

"I'll go and get you a horse," Clint said. "You stay here."

"Why?"

"What happened out there today?"

"Oh, Jesus . . ." Gillett said. "I'm sorry, Clint, but—"

"Did you get dizzy, or did something happen to your eyes?"

"I didn't mean for you to get hurt—"

"Jim!"

"Both," Gillett said. "My vision got fuzzy, and I got dizzy."

"Okay," Clint said. "Let the doctor take a look at you while I get you another horse."

"It don't matter what he says," Gillett said. "I'm still going after them."

"We both are, Jim," Clint said, putting his hand on his friend's shoulder, "we both are."

FORTY

Clint found a new horse for Gillett while the Ranger submitted to an examination by the doctor. The best he could do was a sturdy bay mare that he managed to wangle out of the liveryman for sixty dollars.

By the time he returned to the doctor's office the man had finished his examination.

"What do you think, Doc?" Clint asked, glancing at Gillett, who obviously was not happy.

"I'm not an expert in this field, Mr. Adams," the doctor said. "Head injuries are pretty much uncharted territory for me."

"Can you make a guess?"

"The brain is very delicate," he said. "When Mr. Gillett was hit on the head, his brain could have actually bounced off the side of his skull." To illustrate, the doctor reached out and touched the side of Clint's head. "Since he has not taken sufficient time to recover from the injury, this might be why he's experiencing problems with his vision and his balance."

"So you're saying that if he rested, the condition might correct itself?"

"That's what I'm saying," the doctor said, then added, "that is, if the injury is not more extensive than that. I'd suggest you get your friend to someone who specializes in this sort of thing."

"Can you recommend someone?" Clint asked.

"Not really," the doctor said. "My guess is you'd find someone like that in a city like Denver, or San Francisco, or New York."

"Well," Gillett said, standing up, "we ain't going to any of those cities, we're going to a small town called San Genero."

The doctor looked at Gillett and said, "That's up to you, Mr. Gillett. I've done all that I can do."

"And we're grateful to you, Doc," Clint said.

"Did you get my horse?" Gillett asked.

"I got *a* horse, yes," Clint said.

"Then we better get started," Gillett said. "The faster we get to San Genero, the faster we can finally get this over with."

As Clint and Gillett headed for the door, the doctor said, "Do either of you gentlemen know what Mr. Ledbetter is talking about?"

"Ledbetter?" Gillett said.

"The man you shot," the doctor said.

"What about him?" Clint asked.

"He keeps asking me to keep the mob away from him," the doctor said. "Do you know what he's talking about?"

They looked at each other and then Gillett said, "No idea, Doc. Maybe he's got one of them—you know, head injuries?"

Outside the doctor's office Clint had Duke and Gillett's new horse waiting.

"How do you feel?" Clint asked.

"Don't mother me, Clint."

Clint leaned on his saddle and stared across at Gillett.

"Seems to me that I've got a right to."

"Why?" Gillett demanded. "Because I almost got you killed?"

Clint looked at the sky for a moment, then said, "Yeah, that would pretty much give me the right, don't you think?"

"Look," Gillett said, "I'm damn sorry it happened, Clint. Don't give up on me now, though. We've got them this time. I know we do."

"When this is over," Clint said, "you'll either take a long rest, or go see one of those specialists. Agreed?"

"Will you go with me if I agree?"

"Yes."

"Okay," Gillett said. "I'll go."

"Good."

They mounted up and started riding out of town, toward Mexico.

"I would have gone with you even if you hadn't agreed," Clint said moments later.

FORTY-ONE

In San Genero the Baca brothers felt safe. There, with Carlos Montanez, nothing could touch them. This was home to them, which very few people knew. They had grown up here, and years ago had killed their first woman here.

She'd hardly been a woman. They had been sixteen and she a lovely girl of fifteen. When the Bacas finished with her, though, she was no longer lovely—or alive.

They left San Genero then, in disgrace, but now it was ten years later, and the people of San Genero feared the Bacas too much to condemn them—openly or otherwise—for what they had done years ago—and what they were still doing.

One man, however, was not afraid. That was the local priest, Father Damien. Father Damien was forty years old when the Bacas had killed Angelina Mendez. Now he was fifty, and the memory of how

163

she looked—battered, broken, and dead—was still vivid in his mind.

When he saw the Bacas ride in the day before, he had spit on the ground and then asked God for forgiveness. It was true the Lord forgave all, but Father Damien hoped that, in His infinite wisdom, God would never forgive the Bacas for what they had done to Angelina—let alone to however many women they had brutalized or killed during the ensuing ten years.

In the local cantina, the Bacas sat with Carlos Montanez.

"When the others get here," Abran said, "we will plan our next job."

When the Bacas were not killing women, they were robbing banks, or stages, or trains, or anyone they thought might have money.

"They should be here soon," Montanez said.

"At the most we'll have to wait three days," Abran said. "If the Ranger has not reached Chapman by then, that will mean he finally lost our trail."

"What will we do if we ever meet up with him again?" Enofre said.

"You remember that sheriff in Never Bend?" Abran asked his brother.

"Oh, yes," Enofre said, his eyes shining. He also remembered the little blond whore. She had reminded him of Angelina Mendez. True, Angelina had been dark-haired and olive-skinned while the whore had been blond and pale, but physically they were the same. Physically, they were *all* the same, the women he had killed since Angelina.

In point of fact, over the years Enofre had been having Angelina time and time again.

Abran, on the other hand, even at sixteen, had liked larger, heavier women—like Angelina's mother, Amparo. Amparo Mendez had been fourteen years old when she gave birth to Angelina, so she had only been twenty-nine ten years ago. At twenty-eight she had first taken the fifteen-year-old Abran to her bed and initiated him into the ways of sex. That went on for five months before she tossed him away. Well, he showed her, didn't he? He had helped Enofre lure young Angelina away from the house, away from her mother and drunken, useless father, and then Enofre had initiated Angelina.

"Have you seen Amparo?" Montanez asked.

"No," Abran said, "not yet. I will go over there later. Let her wait for me."

Whenever Abran and Enofre returned to San Genero, he went to see Amparo. At thirty-nine she was still a full-bodied beauty. Even though she knew that Abran had helped Enofre kill her daughter, she was too frightened of them to reject Abran's advances.

Five years ago they had returned and Abran had also killed her husband, who had walked in on them in bed. Drunk, he had tried to act like a husband for the first time in his life, and Abran had calmly shot him from the bed, and then continued to have sex with Amparo with the body of her husband on the floor by the bed.

"Later," Abran said, but even now he felt his penis thickening at the thought of her. What was it about her, he wondered, that drew him to her? Was it that he knew she hated him? Or was it that she had been his first woman?

He didn't know. He only knew that he never felt the urge with her, not *that* urge. It was only when he was away from San Genero that he felt it.

Enofre, on the other hand, felt it even here, but so far Abran had been able to keep his brother in check the times they had been back here. He had not killed a woman in San Genero since Angelina Mendez.

Abran hoped to keep it that way.

Father Damien sat in his church and cursed himself for a coward. He was harsh with himself when it came to the Bacas. He could not abide them and should long ago have left San Genero so he would not have to deal with them. He could not bring himself to leave, though. He could not leave his people, his flock. They needed him—even more so when Abran and Enofre Baca came back.

Begging forgiveness from his Savior once again, Father Damien prayed that someone would come to San Genero and rid them of this disease, this pestilence known as Abran and Enofre Baca.

FORTY-TWO

When Clint Adams and James Gillett rode into San
Genero, the first building they passed was a small
adobe church. As they started past it, the front door
opened and a priest came running out, waving to
them.

"What's he want, I wonder?" Gillett asked.

"Let's find out," Clint said.

They stopped and waited for the priest to reach
them.

"*Señors*," the man said, "I saw you from the church . . .
I saw the badge on your shirt. Are you officers of
the law?"

"I am a Texas Ranger, Father," Gillett said. "This man
is simply a friend of mine. What can we do for you?"

"You can answer my prayers, *señor*," the priest said,
"if you tell me that you are here because of Abran and
Enofre Baca."

Clint and Gillett exchanged glances.

"How did you know that, Father?" Gillett asked.

The priest clasped his hands in front of him and said, "I did not know, *señor*, but I have been praying for someone to come and rid San Genero of them. God forgive me, those men deserve to die and serve the Devil himself in hell."

"That's strong talk, Father," Clint said.

"Alas," the priest said, "all I am able to do is talk. I cannot defend my town, my people, against them. They come and go whenever they want, take what they want, and then leave us with the hope that they will not return—and then they do."

"Why do they keep coming back here?" Gillett asked.

"They were born here," the priest said, "and grew up here."

"Then you know them personally, Father?" Gillett asked.

"May God forgive me for cursing the day I baptized them both," he said.

"Father . . . what's your name?" Clint asked.

"Father Damien."

"Father Damien," Clint said, "perhaps we can help each other in this matter. May we speak to you?"

Father Damien took Clint and Gillett into the church and spoke to them at length about Abran and Enofre Baca. They then told him what the Baca brothers had been up to north of the border.

"Then they are even worse than I feared," Father Damien said. "*Señors*, I always hoped that I would never know a man who was pure evil—but I have known two of them. Please, have you come to take them away with you?"

"Either that," Gillett said, "or kill them."

Father Damien looked at Gillett for a few moments, and then pointed at him and said, "You have some . . . personal score to settle with these men, do you not?"

"I have," Gillett said. "Does it show?"

"Oh, yes," Father Damien said, "I can see it in your eyes, *señor*. You will kill them, I think."

"If they force me to."

"No," Father Damien said, "you will kill them—and you will feel no guilt afterward."

"If I kill them," Gillett said, "you're right, I won't feel any guilt."

"Well, my son," Father Damien said, "they have done you a great wrong, and you have vengeance in your heart. When you have done what you have come to do, you must come and speak with me. The Lord will forgive you, my son, but you must ask Him for His forgiveness."

"I'm really not that concerned with forgiveness, Father," Gillett said, standing up. "No disrespect intended."

"None taken, my son," Father Damien said, walking them to the front door, "but remember what I said. I will be here waiting."

"I'll remember, Father. Can you tell us where to find them?"

"Most likely in the cantina," Father Damien said. "They have rooms above it."

"Thanks, Father."

Gillett went outside, and Father Damien put his hand on Clint's arm to stop him.

"You are his friend?"

"Yes."

"Will you try to stop him?"

"I'll back his play, Father," Clint said. "My concern is that he doesn't get killed."

"You have no animosity toward these men?"

"They have not harmed me personally, Father," Clint said, "but I can't say that I don't, no. I have heard what they've done, and I don't want them to do it anymore."

"Your motives, they are more pure than your friend's," Father Damien said. "Justice, rather than vengeance. Still, if you kill them, I make you the same offer I made Mr. Gillett. Come here and talk to me."

"I'll remember, Father."

Outside the church, Gillett was already mounted and ready to go.

"What did he want to say to you?" he asked as Clint mounted up.

"He wanted to see if my motives were more pure than yours."

"He didn't like my motives, huh?" Gillett asked. "That won't stop him from being happy when we've gotten rid of the Baca brothers."

"I guess not."

"And were they?"

"What?"

"Your motives?" Gillett asked. "Did he think they were more pure than mine?"

"He seemed to think so."

"What does that mean?" Gillett asked. "I'll need forgiveness and you won't?"

"Oh, no," Clint said, "I'll go to hell, same as you, if I don't pray for forgiveness."

"How do you feel about that?" Gillett asked. "Are you a religious man?"

"Not particularly."

"So how do you feel about what the Father said?" he asked.

"Hey," Clint said, "I signed on to see this through to the end—even if the end is hell."

"All right, then," Gillett said, "let's go and see where this is going to end."

FORTY-THREE

At that moment the Baca brothers were not in the same place.

Enofre Baca was in the cantina, eating and drinking and trying not to give in to the urge, which was becoming insistent. Abran had warned him that they could not give in to the urge while in San Genero, and that they would be leaving town shortly.

Enofre, however, was having difficulty controlling his feelings, and the amount of whiskey he was drinking was not helping.

Soon, he knew, the urge would be too powerful for him to resist, and there was nothing anybody could do about it.

Abran Baca was with Amparo Mendez. He had the older woman on her hands and knees on her bed and was on his knees behind her. He ran his hands over the firm, round cheeks of her butt, then slid one hand between her thighs so that he could probe her with his finger. She was wet and hot, and moaned in what he chose to take as a sound of appreciation.

He probed her with his middle finger, then inserted a second finger and began to stimulate her that way. She pressed back against the pressure of his hand.

Amparo Mendez hated the Baca brothers. Enofre had killed her daughter, and Abran had killed her husband. That was why she felt shame whenever Abran came to her and took her. She felt shame because her body always responded to his touch, no matter how rough it was. While her body was filled with pleasure from the way he took her, her brain was pleading for forgiveness from God, because she was trying to summon the strength to kill herself once Abran had left her. As was always the case, though, she did not have the courage to do so.

Abran abruptly removed his hand from her and roughly spread her thighs wider. She felt his rigid penis slide between her firm thighs and then enter her. He drove into her forcefully, grabbing hold of her hips and pulling her back toward him. As he began to slide in and out of her, she felt the pleasure rising up to render her mindless, and suddenly she was crying out, imploring the man who, with his brother, had wiped out her family—imploring him on, begging him to fulfill her and at the same time wishing that the Lord would choose that very moment to strike them both dead.

Abran Baca loved the way Amparo Mendez smelled when he took her this way. Her thick woman smell and the odor of her perspiration excited him more and more. He knew that her body responded to him, even

while her mind cursed him, but he didn't care. It was
her body he wanted—he had *always* wanted it, ever
since he was a youth, and it had been the same with
them over the past ten years, since the first time she
had taken him to her bed. Once he had learned, he had
immediately taken control of her. Even though she was
older, and she had been the teacher, it was he who—
even at sixteen and certainly now—was the master.

He ran his hands over her back as he pounded into
her, reached around to cup her large, swaying breasts,
pinched her nipples so hard that she cried out in pleasure
and pain, and then he leaned over and *bit* her on the
shoulder, causing her to scream. . . .

Downstairs Enofre heard the woman scream and
knew that it was coming from his brother's room.
In that moment the urge coursed through him, and
he stood up quickly, knocking over his chair in the
process.

It was time for him to go out and find a young girl,
one who would remind him of his Angelina.

It was time for him to have Angelina, again.

Clint and Gillett were riding up the street when
they, too, heard the scream of the woman.

They exchanged quick glances and headed for the
cantina.

"I don't know what that sounded like to you," Clint
said, "but it *could* be a couple of things."

"I know what you're thinking," Gillett said, "and
if we're making a mistake, we'll apologize to both
the man and the woman for interrupting their pleasure.

Meanwhile, there's the chance that we just might be saving somebody's life."

They dismounted as the woman screamed again, and this time—at least, to Clint—it sounded like a woman who was being pleasured, not tortured.

Still . . .

"Front or back?" Clint asked Gillett.

"I'll take the front," the Ranger said. "The back is yours."

"With any luck," Clint said, "we'll both come out of this alive and meet halfway."

"Good luck, then."

"To you, too, pard."

FORTY-FOUR

Enofre Baca staggered toward the front door of the cantina, hitching up his gun belt as he went. Before he reached it, however, it opened and a man stepped in—a man wearing a Texas Ranger's badge.

"You!"

"You know who I am?" Gillett asked.

"You are the Ranger."

"Which one are you?" Gillett asked.

"I am Enofre."

"I guess it doesn't matter really," Gillett went on, "since you both look alike, and you're both sick."

Enofre frowned and asked, "What do you have against us? Why have you followed us?"

"You don't know, do you?"

"No," Enofre said, looking puzzled.

"I guess to you what you do is normal," Gillett said, "but to others it's sick. To the friends and families of the women you've killed—the *girls*—it's perverted and devastating."

Enofre frowned again and asked, "What does that mean?"

Gillett shook his head and said, "It means it's time to die."

Clint went around the back and found a way in. Once inside he located the stairs that led to the second floor. Once upstairs it wasn't hard to locate the room because the woman wasn't the only one making noise now; the man was, too.

Clint stood in front of the door and hoped that he wasn't just interrupting some whore at work.

He kicked the door, and it slammed open.

"*Hijo de un cabrón!*" Enofre Baca swore, and went for his gun.

Gillett was not a fast gun—certainly not as fast as Clint Adams—but he had done this enough times to know that the surest shot was the safest shot.

He kept his head and while Enofre was drunkenly trying to grope his gun from his holster, Gillett drew his gun cleanly and fired once. The bullet punched Enofre in the chest, driving him back a step. A surprised look came over his face and he opened his mouth to speak.

Calmly—but knowing that this was for his sister and the woman he loved—Gillett pulled the trigger again . . . and again . . . and again . . . and kept pulling it until the hammer clicked several times on the empty chambers.

•   •   •

Abran Baca leapt off the woman and off the bed and instinctively grabbed for his gun, which was hanging on the bedpost.

The woman was naked, slick with perspiration and bleeding from several bites on her shoulders. Clint saw her in the blink of an eye, then turned his attention to the man. He had no time to ask if he was one of the Bacas, but the blood on the woman convinced him that he was. Also, the man *was* going for his gun, and whoever he was, he was obviously planning to shoot Clint.

Clint drew his gun and fired. The first bullet struck the man high in the back on the left side and drove through. Blood and chunks of flesh struck the wall and stuck there.

The force of the shot drove the man into the wall face first and he slid to the floor, breathing raggedly.

"Is this one of the Bacas?" Clint asked the woman.

She didn't answer, at first. She was staring at the wounded man.

"*Señorita!*" Clint shouted, getting her attention.

"*Sí?*" she asked, her eyes wide. Some of the man's blood had landed on her, speckling her skin.

"Is he a Baca? Enofre? Or Abran?"

"*Sí, sí!*" she said, holding the sheet up in front of her now. "*Ésta Abran Baca!*"

Clint looked at the man and saw him start to reach for his gun again. The gun belt was hanging from the bedpost, still within his reach.

"You've killed your last woman, Baca," he said and shot the man in the head.

● ● ●

GILLETT'S RANGERS   179

Clint paused only to check that Abran Baca was dead, then told the woman to get dressed. She thanked him profusely. Clint did not know exactly what her relationship to Abran Baca had been, but she did not seem sad that the man was dead. In fact, she took the opportunity to spit on his dead body.

He walked downstairs, hoping that the barrage of shots he had heard had come mostly from Gillett's gun.

When he reached the cantina, he saw a man lying on the floor, a man who looked exactly like the man he'd killed upstairs.

Gillett was at the bar with a bottle of whiskey in his hand. The bartender behind the bar looked frightened, too frightened to move.

"That's Enofre," the Ranger said.

"Abran's upstairs," Clint said, "dead."

As Clint approached Gillett, the Ranger held out the whiskey bottle and said, "A little late, but Merry Christmas."

Clint accepted the bottle and said, "Hell of a Christmas."

"Sí," the bartender said to both of them. "Feliz Navidad!"

Watch for

RETURN TO DEADWOOD

146th novel in the exciting GUNSMITH series
from Jove

Coming in February!

A special offer for people who enjoy reading the best Westerns published today.

WESTERNS!

NO OBLIGATION

Mail the coupon below

To start your subscription and receive 2 FREE WESTERNS, fill out the coupon below and mail it today. We'll send your first shipment which includes 2 FREE BOOKS as soon as we receive it.

Mail To: **True Value Home Subscription Services, Inc. P.O. Box 5235 120 Brighton Road, Clifton, New Jersey 07015-5235**

YES! I want to start reviewing the very best Westerns being published today. Send me my first shipment of 6 Westerns for me to preview FREE for 10 days. If I decide to keep them, I'll pay for just 4 of the books at the low subscriber price of $2.75 each; a total $11.00 (a $21.00 value). Then each month I'll receive the 6 newest and best Westerns to preview Free for 10 days. If I'm not satisfied I may return them within 10 days and owe nothing. Otherwise I'll be billed at the special low subscriber rate of $2.75 each; a total of $16.50 (at least a $21.00 value) and save $4.50 off the publishers price. There are never any shipping, handling or other hidden charges. I understand I am under no obligation to purchase any number of books and I can cancel my subscription at any time, no questions asked. In any case the 2 FREE books are mine to keep.

Name _____

Street Address _____ Apt. No. _____

City _____ State _____ Zip Code _____

Telephone _____

Signature _____

(if under 18 parent or guardian must sign)

Terms and prices subject to change. Orders subject to acceptance by True Value Home Subscription Services, Inc.

11285-2